# A Rancher
# for Christmas

## Brenda Minton

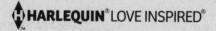

Recycling programs for this product may not exist in your area.

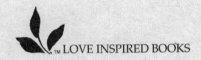 ™ LOVE INSPIRED BOOKS

ISBN-13: 978-0-373-81805-1

A Rancher for Christmas

Copyright © 2014 by Brenda Minton

www.Harlequin.com

Printed in U.S.A.

Not that I speak in respect of want:
for I have learned, in whatsoever state I am,
therewith to be content.
— *Philippians* 4:11

Dedicated to my sweet ladies at the residential care facility. Your prayers, hugs and love have meant so much to me. Lola, this one is for you.

And to friends who are always just a phone call away. Pam, Lori, Tracie, Steph and Shirlee.

Melissa Endlich, as always, thank you!

# Chapter One

Breezy Hernandez stood in front of the massive wood door on the front porch of her brother's Texas Hill Country home. When she'd met Lawton Brooks two months ago, he had filled in the missing pieces of her life.

Now he was gone. In one tragic accident Lawton, his wife and his mother had been taken. The lawyer in Austin had given her this address. He'd told her in Martin's Crossing she would find Jake Martin, executor of the estate.

She knocked on the door and then looked out at the windblown fields dotted with small trees, waiting for someone to answer. No one did. There was no muffled call for her to come in, or footsteps hurrying to answer the door. She leaned her forehead against the rough wood, her hand dropping to her side. Her heart ached.

After a few minutes she wiped away the

dampness on her cheeks and reached for the handle. It wasn't locked. She pushed the door open, hesitating briefly before stepping inside. Why should she hesitate? Nothing would change the reality that Lawton and his wife had been killed in a plane crash two weeks ago. She'd missed the opportunity to see him again. She'd missed the funeral and the chance to say goodbye.

But she could be there for his girls.

As she stepped inside she flipped a switch, flooding the stone-tiled foyer in soft amber light. The entryway led to a massive living room with stone flooring, textured walls in earthy tan and a stone fireplace flanked by brown leather furniture.

Enveloped by silence and the cool, unheated air, she stood in the center of the room. There were signs of life, as if the people who had lived here had just stepped out. There were magazines on the coffee table, a pair of slippers next to a chair. Toys spilled from a basket pushed against the wall. Her throat tightened, aching deep down the way grief does.

"It isn't fair," she said out loud, the words sounding hollow in the empty space.

She should have come to Texas sooner but she'd needed time to come to terms with what Lawton had told her. His father, Senator Howard

Brooks, had an affair with her mother, Anna, a drug addict from Oklahoma City. Breezy was the result of that brief relationship. She'd known for years that she wasn't the true granddaughter of Maria Hernandez, the woman who had taken her in years ago. Maria had given her that information shortly before she passed away.

Now she knew who she was. But what good did that do her?

She left the living room and walked to the kitchen. The room was large and open, with white cabinets and black granite countertops. She moved from that room, with sippy cups in a drainer next to the sink, to the dining room.

A table with four chairs and two high chairs dominated the room. On the opposite wall were family portraits. She stopped at the picture of an older man in a suit, a flag of Texas behind him. Her father, Senator Howard Brooks.

In the next picture his wife of over forty years stood next to him. They looked happy. Evelyn Brooks hadn't known about her husband's brief affair or his daughter. He'd confessed the secret on his deathbed one year ago.

Breezy drew in a breath and fought the sting of tears. She'd never been one to cry over spilled milk. Not even if that meant she might have had a real family.

This was different, though. This was a family

lost. Her family. She had a habit of losing family. It had started more than twenty years ago, after her mother's death, when she and her siblings were all separated. Mia was adopted by the Coopers and Juan went to his father's family. Breezy had been taken in the night by Maria because she had worried they would eventually learn the truth, that Maria's son wasn't really Breezy's father.

Out of fear, Maria had kept them moving from town to town, living in cars, shelters and sometimes pay-by-the-month hotels.

Breezy brushed off the memory. It was old news.

A wedding photo hung on the wall. She studied the image of her brother and his pretty bride, both wearing identical looks of joy. At the last picture her heart stilled. Lawton, his wife, their two baby girls.

Just then, a sound edged in, a door closing. Footsteps, heavy and booted, echoed in the empty house. She held her breath, waiting.

"Who are you?" The deep male voice sent a shiver of apprehension up her spine.

Breezy turned, not quite trembling in her shoes, but nearly. The man filled the doorway. His tall, lean frame in jeans and a dark blue shirt held her attention, and then her eyes connected with pale blue eyes in a suntanned face.

His dark hair was short but messy, like he'd just taken off a hat. She let her gaze drop, almost expecting a holster, Old West style, slung low on his hips.

Of course there wasn't one.

"I'm Breezy. Breezy Hernandez." Chin up, she swallowed a lump of what might have been fear.

His eyes narrowed and he frowned. "The missing sister."

She wanted to argue she hadn't been missing. She hadn't known she was lost. She'd needed time to process that she had this brother. She'd needed time alone to figure out what it meant to find out who her father was. The ache in her heart erupted again. She'd been on the run for most of her life; it had become second nature to take off when things got a little dicey. Maria Hernandez had taught her that.

"So we know who I am. Who are you?" She managed to not shake as she asked the question, meeting his somewhat intimidating gaze.

"Jake Martin."

"Of Martin's Crossing." The town in the middle of nowhere that she'd driven through to get here.

"Yes, Martin's Crossing."

"The girls?" She glanced back over her shoulder and saw that he was moving toward her.

"They're safe." He stepped close, smelling of the outdoors, fresh country air and soap. "I got a call from Brock, the attorney in Austin. He said he told you to come here and talk to me."

"Yes, he told me about Lawton and asked me to find you." She shook her head. "I missed the funeral, I'm sorry."

She didn't give him explanations.

She guessed the Goliath standing in front of her wouldn't want to hear explanations. He wouldn't want to know how much it hurt to know that all these years she'd had another brother. And now he was gone.

"Right." He looked away, but not before she saw the sorrow flash across his face, settling in his eyes. She started to reach out but knew she shouldn't. Her hand remained at her side.

Maybe they were feeling the same sense of loss but he didn't seem to be a man who wanted comfort from a stranger. From her.

"So, you came for your inheritance?" He dropped the words, sharp and insulting.

"Is that why you think I'm here?"

"It would make sense."

She shook her head. "No, it doesn't. It's insulting."

He shrugged one powerful shoulder. "Your brother was my best friend. His daughters are my nieces. I have every right to keep them safe."

"I'm not here for any reason other than to see them." She turned and walked back to the kitchen.

"Running?" He followed her, light on his feet for a man so large.

"Not at all. I need a minute to cool off so I don't hit you with something."

At that, the smooth planes of his face shifted and he smiled. She was slammed with a myriad of other emotions that seemed more dangerous than her rage. At the sink she filled a glass with water and took a sip. He scooted a chair out from the island in the middle of the big room and bent his large form to fit the seat. She ignored the lethal way he sat, like a wild cat about to attack. She ignored that he had beautiful features, strong but beautiful. She could draw him, or chisel his likeness in stone.

Or grab a chunk of granite and…

His eyebrows lifted, as if he guessed where her thoughts had gone.

"I'm not here to take what I can and leave." She remained standing on the opposite side of the island, not wanting to be anywhere near him. She needed that force of wood and stone between them.

"Really." His voice was smooth but deep, and full of skepticism.

"Yes, really. I had a father and a brother that

I never got to meet. I wanted to come here because this is where Lawton lived. I thought I might somehow…" She shook her head. "Never mind. He's gone. I want to meet his daughters. Please, just let me meet them."

Jake stood, rethinking what he'd come to tell her. Rethinking her. She stood on the other side of the counter, as if the granite could protect her. As he eased out of the chair, she moved a little to the right, her back against the counter. Brown eyes the unfortunate color of caramel watched him.

Unfortunate because her eyes were strangely compelling. And more, there were emotions that flickered in their depths—sadness, anger, loss. He hadn't expected to feel anything for her other than distrust.

"I'm going to get a glass of water, nothing else," he said.

He opened the cabinet and found a glass, filling it with cold water from the fridge. He took a drink and studied the sister of his best friend, looking for similarities. She had long straight dark blond hair that framed a face that he'd call beautiful but strong. She was tall and slim but not thin. The peasant skirt and blouse gave her a bohemian look. She would stand out in Martin's

Crossing. If she stayed. He doubted she would. She had city written all over her.

Yes, she looked enough like Lawton for him to believe she was his sister. Lawton had obviously believed it. Even before the DNA test.

"Well?" she asked.

"You remind me of your brother."

"I hope that's a compliment."

"It's an observation." He watched her, still unsure. He'd been unsure from the beginning when Lawton first told him about her. "I need to head back to my place. You can meet me over there."

Jake poured out the remaining water and put the glass in the dishwasher. She had moved away from him again. He didn't comment, just walked past her and headed for the front door, grabbing his hat off the hook on his way out. She followed.

He had more on his mind than a sister who suddenly showed up when it looked as if the gravy train might have derailed in her front yard. Back at his place he had a mare about to foal. He'd lost a good cow that morning and now had a calf to tend to. He had fifty head of cattle heading to the sale tomorrow and a brother who couldn't get his act together.

They both stopped on the porch. The temperature, typical of late November, had dropped fifteen degrees while they'd been inside. Clouds were rolling, gray and full of rain.

"How far?" She looked past him to the open land and seemed unsure. Then she focused her attention on the horse he'd tied to the post.

"Not far." He untied his horse, tightening the girth strap and watching her over the top of the saddle. "Since I'm riding, you'll need to go back down the drive, turn left and in a mile take a left at the entrance to the Circle M."

"How long before you get there?"

"It'll take me a little longer but I'm cutting through the field, so not much." They stood there staring at each other and he noticed the softness in her brown eyes. The last thing he wanted was to give in to the softness. Lawton had immediately trusted her. That wasn't Jake's way. He had to be the one to draw lines and make sure no one got hurt. But he wasn't an ogre. "I'm sorry."

She gave a quick nod her eyes registering surprise. "Thank you."

"He was a good man." More words of kindness. His brother Duke would have been proud. He'd told Jake to be nice to their new sister. He'd almost laughed at that. She was *not* their new sister.

Jake didn't need one more person to watch out

for. His plate was full of siblings that couldn't seem to stay out of trouble.

With a goodbye nod, he put a foot in the stirrup and swung himself into the saddle. She shot him a wary look and headed for her car.

He watched her go, holding the gray gelding steady as the horse tossed his head, eager to be on his way. The car was down the drive when he turned the horse and headed for home. The rain had blown over but the air was damp and cool. It felt good, to let Bud loose. The horse was itching to run. So was Jake. But he knew he couldn't outrun the problem that was driving to his place in a compact car with Oklahoma tags.

Fifteen minutes later, with his horse unsaddled and back in the pasture, he headed for the house. Breezy was standing on the front porch of the stone-and-log home he'd been living in alone for more years than he cared to count. He'd be thirty-four soon. He guessed that made him a crusty bachelor.

"Pretty place," Breezy said when he reached the front porch of the house.

"Thank you."

He nodded toward the door. Time to get it over with. He figured she'd be here another ten minutes, and then she'd be gone and he wouldn't have to worry about her. He'd hand her a check and they'd go their separate ways.

Today he'd said a few prayers on the matter and maybe it was wrong, but he'd prayed she'd take the out. Of course he knew God didn't exactly answer prayers based on Jake Martin's wants. But he'd sure be grateful if the good Lord made this easy on him.

"Let's go inside." He led her across the porch with the bentwood furniture. Ceiling fans hung from the porch ceiling and in the summer they made evenings almost bearable. Not that he spent a lot of time sitting out there.

"Do you live here alone?" she asked, turning a bright shade of pink. "I mean, do you have family here? In Martin's Crossing?"

"This is my home and I do have family in Martin's Crossing." He didn't plan on giving her the family history.

What would he tell her? That he and his twin sister had helped raise their younger siblings after their mom had left town, left their dad and them? This ranch had been in their family for over one hundred years and keeping it going had put his dad in an early grave. Now he'd lost his sister, and he was determined to find a way to keep the family together, keep them strong, without her.

But no, he wasn't alone. He had his brothers, Duke and Brody. They had their little sister, Sam. Short for Samantha.

Duke lived in the old family homestead just down the road.

Their little brother, Brody, only came around when he needed a place to heal up after a bad ride on the back of a bull. The rest of the time he stayed with friends in a rented trailer in Stephenville.

Sam had been in boarding school and was now in college. Out of state. That was his idea, after she couldn't seem to keep her mind off a certain ranch hand. Their dad, Gabe Martin, hadn't seemed to connect with the thought that his family was falling apart. It had all been on Jake.

The house was dark and cool. He led Breezy through the living room and down the hall to his office.

He flipped the switch, bathing the room in light, and motioned for her to take a seat. He positioned himself behind the massive oak fixture and pulled out a drawer to retrieve papers.

Breezy took the seat on the other side of the desk. With a hand that trembled, she pushed long blond hair back from her face. Lawton had mentioned she sang and played guitar. Something about being a street performer in California. Jake had taken it upon himself to learn more.

"Why didn't you come back here with Lawton?" Jake asked, pinning her with a look that always made Samantha squirm. He didn't have kids of his own, probably never would, but he knew all the tricks.

She looked away, her attention on the fireplace.

"Miss Hernandez?"

"Call me Breezy," she whispered as she refocused, visibly pulling herself together. "I needed time to come to terms with what he'd told me. I didn't know how to suddenly be the sister he thought I would be. Or could be. And I have a sister in Oklahoma."

"I understand." It had come out of nowhere, this new family of hers. "Lawton's dad kept his skeletons hidden pretty deeply. But as he got older—" he shrugged "—guilt caught up with him."

"I see." She bit down on her bottom lip. "I could have been a part of their lives."

His heart shifted a little. And sympathy was the last thing he wanted to feel.

"Yes, I guess."

"And Lawton's wife. She looked very sweet."

That's when his own pain slammed him hard. He cleared his throat, cleared the lump of emotion that settled there. He hadn't yet gotten used to the loss. "Elizabeth was my twin sister."

She bit down on her bottom lip and closed her eyes, just briefly. "I'm so sorry."

"So am I."

"So why am I here?"

"Because Lawton came home from Oklahoma and changed his will." He brushed a hand over his face, then he reached for the manila envelope on his desk. "He left you his house, money from his dad's estate, as well as a small percentage of his software and technologies company. He left the twins a larger percentage as well as a trust fund. The business manager, Tyler Randall, also inherited a small percentage of the company."

"I see." But she clearly didn't understand. He was about to make it clear. And he prayed she'd take the out.

"Breezy, Lawton and Elizabeth left us joint custody of their daughters."

He and this woman were now parents to two little girls.

# *Chapter Two*

"No." Breezy shook her head. This couldn't be happening. No one would give her custody, even shared custody, of two little girls. "He couldn't have done that."

"I'm afraid he did."

She met his blue gaze, knowing he disliked her. Or at the least, disliked the situation he'd been forced into with her. He knew these little girls. They were the children of his twin sister. Of course he was angry. She was angry, too.

What had made Lawton, a man she barely knew, think this was a good idea? She'd never stayed in one place longer than six months until she moved to Dawson, Oklahoma. She'd never had real family until her sister, Mia, found her. She definitely didn't know how to raise a child.

"I'm not sure what to say," she admitted.

"That makes two of us. I never planned on

losing my sister and my best friend. And I certainly couldn't have seen this coming."

Jake Martin studied her. His blue eyes were sharp; his generous mouth was a straight, unforgiving line.

He shook his head and hit a button on an intercom. A woman answered. "Okay," he said.

She sat quietly, forcing herself to maintain eye contact with him. The door behind her opened. She didn't turn, even when he looked past her, smiling at whoever had entered the room. There were footsteps and quiet voices.

Curiosity overrode her desire to hold his gaze, to not feel weak. She glanced back over her shoulder and the room spun in a crazy way that left her fighting tears, trying to focus. Twin girls toddled across the room wearing identical smiles on identical faces.

"These are your nieces." His voice came from far away.

"Oh." What else could she say? The toddler girls were smiling as they bypassed her to get to Jake Martin.

"The lovely lady behind them is Marty, their nanny," he explained, nodding toward the older woman who had remained in the doorway. He leaned down, holding out his arms. The girls ran to him and climbed onto his lap. He hugged them both tight.

"They're beautiful." They were dark-haired with blue eyes and big smiles. After all they'd been through, they could still smile. Though she didn't want to, she attributed that to the man sitting across from her.

"They are." He kissed the top of each dark head. "And we are their guardians."

"You should have told me."

He shrugged and looked at the girls, who had picked up pens and were drawing on the papers on his desk. He moved the envelope out of their reach.

"I think I just did."

"I meant from the beginning."

"Really? I should have disclosed this to someone I've never met?" He shook his head. "I'll do whatever I need to do to keep them safe."

"I get that." She kept her voice soft, not wanting the girls to hear anger. She had too many memories of loud and unforgiving voices as she hid beneath the bed with Mia and their brother, Juan.

Was she really angry with him? As she studied the little girls on his lap, she thought not. He wanted to protect them.

He grinned at the girls and they reached up to pat his lean cheeks. "Rosie and Violet, this is your aunt Breezy."

She had nieces. She wanted to hug those little girls close. She wanted to hold them forever. They were looking at her, wide-eyed, curious but not ready to come to her.

"Hi, girls." What else could she say? Her vision blurred. She raised her hand to wipe away the tears that drifted down her cheeks.

Jake Martin looked at the little girls he held, his gaze serious and then he refocused on Breezy. He studied her, as if looking for a sign that she might run. He pushed a box of tissues across the desk, never removing his eyes from her. She wouldn't run. She didn't know what he knew about her, about her past, but she wouldn't run. She couldn't. Not now.

"Marty, why don't you take the girls back to their playroom?" He set the girls down, easing them onto their feet. They walked around the desk and Breezy wanted to touch them. Rose smiled up at her and toddled close, little legs and bare feet peeking out from her colorful sundress, white with big brightly colored flowers. Violet held back, letting Rose take the lead.

They were identical, but not. Rose had a slightly rounder face. Her dark hair had a bit of wave. Violet's dark hair was perfectly straight.

"Hi, Rose." She leaned and the little girl walked up, unafraid, her little face splitting in a dimpled grin.

"Hi, Rose," the toddler repeated and giggled. Breezy smiled.

"You're both very pretty."

"Very pretty," Rose repeated and Violet giggled.

"And smart."

"Smart a…" Rose started what sounded like something inappropriate.

"No!" Marty jumped forward. "Uncle Duke is a bad influence."

"I know he is." Jake shook his head. "He's going to start putting money in a college fund if he doesn't watch his language around them."

Marty took the hand of each girl and they left the room with soft words, giggles and the patter of their bare feet.

"They're precious." Breezy turned to face what felt like her judge and jury. He had leaned back in the big leather chair and his booted feet were on the desk.

"Yes, they are. And I will do anything to protect them."

"I'm sure you would." She studied him for a minute. "But you don't have to protect them from me."

"That's the problem. I don't know you, Breezy. I know you were Lawton's sister and he had the crazy idea that this would be best for his girls. But he also didn't plan on dying so soon."

"You don't want me in their lives?"

He exhaled sharply and shook his head. Of course he didn't. "I'm not sure what I want."

The answer surprised her. "Did you hope I wouldn't show up?"

He shrugged. "It would have made my life easier."

"Right, but I'm here and those little girls are just as much my family as they are yours. Tell me what I need to do."

Jake Martin tapped his pen on the desk and studied her.

"Lawton left us joint custody as long as you remain here, in his house. But there are stipulations. If you leave, you lose custody and ownership of the house. If I see a reason that you're not capable of this, I take full custody. If either of those should happen and I should take full custody, the house goes to the girls. The money is yours no matter what happens. He had hoped…"

"That I would be in their lives."

"Yes. He said you'd lived a life of independence and adventure. He wanted his daughters to learn that from you." He brushed his hands through his hair and she saw the lines of exhaustion around his eyes. "Lawton had a very different life. *Structure* was the senator's favorite word."

"I see." She let her gaze travel to the windows that offered a view of the rolling fields dotted with cattle. Craggy, tree-covered hills rose in the distance, gray and misty, as clouds spread across the sky.

Her brother had seen her life as adventurous. She guessed it had been, if a person wasn't fond of knowing where one would sleep or where their next meal would come from.

Jake moved in his chair. His shoulders were broad, his arms corded with strong muscles. Breezy had always been taller than average. She wasn't a petite little thing who backed down easily. She had street smarts, and a black belt.

All of that aside, Jake Martin intimidated her. He was lethal, she thought. The type of man who had always had power, never felt afraid or out of control of his life.

"I guess you'll have to trust me," she said after several minutes of trying to get a handle on her emotions.

"You have the option to take your money and leave." He slid a check and a few papers across the desk.

She took both and he sat there like a rock, a solid mountain of a man with a strong chin and a mouth that shifted the smooth planes of his face when he smiled, making him less intimidating.

She considered the offer, to take the money and leave. That was the option he wanted her to take. And maybe he had the right of it. How long could she stay here without feeling caged? What about her life in Dawson with Mia and her adopted family, the Coopers? Did those two little girls really need someone like her?

Martin's Crossing was another small town. For a girl raised in cities, she wasn't used to small-town closeness, church on Sundays, people who knew her story. A picture of those two little girls on his desk caught her attention, making her rethink who she used to be and forcing her come to terms with the person she needed to be now.

"I'm not going anywhere." She sat back and gave him a satisfied smile that trembled at the edges. Hopefully he didn't notice it, or how her hands shook as she took the check and looked at the amount. She repeated her mantra. "I'm staying here with my nieces. If this is what Lawton wanted, then I owe it to him."

"For how long?" His jaw clenched. "What would it take to buy you out, to make you leave?"

"I'm not for sale. I have two nieces who have lost both of their parents."

He sighed and stood up, obviously not happy with her response.

"Okay, fine. So here's the deal, Breezy." He walked to the window and then looked back at her. "I don't want the girls to be upset by this situation. They've been through enough."

"I agree."

"That means you'll understand that I make the rules."

"Why is that?"

"Several reasons. Lawton left the decision-making to me. They're comfortable with me, and with Marty. I'll bring them over to the house so they can get to know you."

"Joint custody?" she reminded him with a voice that unfortunately shook.

"Right, and that will happen. But first we'll go slowly. You'll visit with them. I'll supervise. If all goes well, we'll come up with an arrangement that works for us both."

"When do I get to spend time with them?"

"Tomorrow." He picked up the hat he'd dropped on his desk. "I have work to get done and you'd probably like to settle in."

"I guess that's my cue to leave." She stood, picking up her purse and waiting for him to say something.

He rounded his desk and walked with her to the door. "I'm sure you'll find what you need at Lawton's place." He pulled a key out of his pocket and handed it to her. "Anything else you need, you'll find in Martin's Crossing."

"Is there a grocery store?"

"Yes. Grocery store, gas station, restaurant and feed store. There are a couple of little shops, antiques and the like."

He opened the front door and motioned her out ahead of him. She shivered as she stepped outside, surprised by how cold it had gotten. With this weather, she could believe Christmas was coming. She'd been looking forward to spending the holidays with Mia.

"Do you have any other questions?" Jake asked.

"None." She nodded at him, her final goodbye. And then the case of nerves she'd been fighting hit and she couldn't get her feet to move forward.

Her brother and sister-in-law were gone. She had two nieces who needed her. She needed them just as much. The man standing next to her seemed to be calling all of the shots. Everything inside her ached.

"Are you okay?" His voice rumbled close to her ear. She shivered at his nearness.

"Yeah, I'm good." She swiped at her eyes and looked away from his steady gaze, taking a deep breath. A hand, strong and warm, touched her arm, sharing his strength.

"It'll all work out. Maybe it doesn't seem that way right now, but it will. And I'm sorry, that you and Lawton didn't have a chance to spend more time together."

She nodded and closed her eyes. The hand remained on her arm. But then it slipped away. She opened her eyes and took in a deep breath. She could do this.

"Thank you." She looked up at him, surprised by the way his presence gave her more strength than she would have imagined.

Maybe someday they would be friends, even allies.

He pulled a business card out of his shirt pocket and a pen, quickly writing something on the back before handing it to her. "That's the information for the alarm system. And you can call if you have any problems. I'll see you tomorrow at noon."

She took the card, glanced at it then slipped it into her purse. "I'll make lunch."

He gave her a look but then he nodded. "You can do that."

Breezy walked down the stone steps to her car, her mind reeling. As she backed out of the drive Jake Martin still stood on the porch. He raised a hand as she pulled away and she returned the gesture.

It was the beginning of a truce. Truce, but not trust. Jake Martin wasn't the type of man who would give trust easily. She understood because she was the same way.

Jake walked back inside. He found Marty waiting for him.

"Are the girls down for a nap?" he asked on his way to the kitchen, knowing Marty would follow.

"Yes. They were asking again." She shook her head, and he knew that meant the girls wanted their mommy and daddy. "They're a little lost, of course."

Jake tossed his hat on the counter as he went for a glass of iced tea. "Aren't we all?"

"Yes, but I worry about you, Jake, about you taking on one more burden."

He shook his head at that. "The twins are family, not a burden."

"You've raised a family. You've been taking care of people your whole life."

Of course, he'd raised a family. His brothers and sisters had been counting on him for as long as he could remember. He'd made sure they were fed. He'd been the one to hire Marty years ago when his dad was sick and not really paying attention. He'd made sure the ranch kept making a profit.

Now he'd make sure Rosie and Violet were loved and protected.

Marty handed him a cup of coffee and then patted his arm the way she'd been doing for a long time, since she and her husband first came to town. Long before she was the cook and housekeeper, she'd figured out what life was like at the Circle M for a bunch of ragtag kids trying to make do with a mom that had left and a dad who had checked out.

"Brody called," she said as she moved back to the counter and a bag of carrots that suddenly held her interest.

"And?" His younger brother had a knack for finding trouble.

"He and Lincoln had a fight. He's coming home."

Brody and his roommate and traveling partner were always one argument away from killing each other so Jake wasn't surprised. He shrugged and took a drink from his cup. Marty started peeling carrots again.

"Well, I guess he'll figure it out. The bull-riding season is almost over. He's probably tired of being on the road."

"He does get homesick, even if he doesn't admit it."

He set the glass in the sink and leaned a hip against the edge of the counter, crossing his arms over his chest as he waited for Marty to tell him what he needed to do. She was good at giving him advice. And, even if he wouldn't admit it, she was usually right.

"Don't lecture him," she finally said. "I heard something in his voice."

"I'll go easy on him. He's a grown man. It's time he made his own decisions, anyway."

Marty put a hand on his arm. "Is it really possible for you to do that?"

He grinned at her fairly unsympathetic tone. "No, probably not. What's for dinner?"

"I'm making beef stew."

"Okay." He waited, watching. He could see the furrow in her brow and knew she had more on her mind than the stew.

"It's okay for you to let this young woman help. I know you have reservations…"

"Because we don't know her at all," he reminded.

Marty shot him a look that he couldn't fail to understand. He was being too "Jake" for her liking. He did like to take control. He liked to know his family was taken care of and safe. Old habits were hard to let go of.

"You've raised your siblings. Now you're looking at raising two little girls. And I'm sorry, but they need more than you, Jake. I think Lawton was right. These girls need Breezy. I might not know her well, but I think I'm a good judge of character and she seems like someone you can trust."

"It's possible she won't stay."

Marty stopped dicing up an onion. "Because of her childhood? All I see is a young woman that was a victim of her situation."

He grinned and kissed the top of Marty's head. "I love you, Marty."

She sniffled and wiped at tears trickling down her cheeks. "Silly onions."

"Onions never make you cry."

"Oh, hush. Go to town."

As Marty cried, he placed a hand on her shoulder. She covered that hand with her own.

"I'm okay."

"Of course you are."

She was always okay. He'd known Marty most of his life. She and her husband had moved to Martin's Crossing to pastor the Community Church at the edge of town. That had been close to twenty-five years ago. After Earl passed away, Marty had stayed on. She'd been the cook and housekeeper for the Martins. Then she'd gone to work for Lawton and Elizabeth after the girls were born.

"I need potatoes," Marty said on a sigh.

"I'll get a bag in town."

"I should have planned better."

He shrugged it off. "I'm sure there are other things we need. I've got a calf to check on, then I'll come back in for a list."

As he reached for his hat, she stopped him. "Give her a chance. I don't think she's had a lot of them."

"That's the Marty I know and love. You always see the good in people."

"This is the Marty who knows that God doesn't need us to judge for Him. That doesn't mean she gets a free pass. Our baby girls come first."

He laughed at that. "And there's the Marty who protects her little ones."

Her smile returned, settling in her gray eyes. "You'd better believe it."

Jake believed it.

And he'd do his best to give Breezy a chance. But flat-out trust? That was something he'd have to work on. He'd learned—in life and in business—to reserve the right to form opinions at a later date.

Time would tell, he told himself as he headed out to the barn. She'd stay or she'd go. While she was in Martin's Crossing he'd do his best to treat her like family, because that's what Lawton would have wanted.

# Chapter Three

Breezy was standing on the porch when Jake pulled up to Lawton's house the next day. She could see two little girls in the backseat of the truck. Her heart thumped hard against her ribs. This was it. Her new life.

She'd spent the rest of yesterday and this morning wondering how she would do this. How would she stay in Martin's Crossing? How would she know how to take care of two little girls? After cleaning a layer of dust off the furniture the previous evening, she'd sat down and tried to list the pros and cons of staying in Martin's Crossing.

And she'd gotten stuck on Jake Martin, on the wariness in his eyes, on the way he'd questioned her, on the way his hand had touched her arm. Jake Martin had trust issues. Breezy had her own issues. She didn't know how to settle, how to put down roots.

Sticking around now took on a lot of importance, for herself and for two little girls. She watched Jake unbuckle the girls from their car seats. Staying meant everything. She headed his way to help.

If he would let her.

It shouldn't bother her. She'd grown up used to people giving her suspicious looks. She'd spent her life adjusting to new people, new situations. She knew how to reinvent herself. She could be the person two little girls needed her to be. Once she figured out who that person was.

She stepped close to the car, watching as he unbuckled one of the twins. Then he placed that little person in her arms. Dark hair straight, face thinner than the other little girl. "Hello, Violet."

The little girl just stared, her eyes big and unsure. Yes, Breezy was getting used to that look. It mirrored the expression on Uncle Jake's face. The man in question pushed the truck door closed. He held Rose in one arm against his side and the little girl patted his cheek with her tiny hand. Breezy watched the change that took place when he was in the presence of these little girls.

The twins made him human. They softened the distrust in his blue eyes.

"Are you ready for us?" he asked with a grin that surprised her.

Breezy nodded. "I'm ready."

She walked in front of him, Violet in her arms. The little girl smelled like baby soap and fabric softener. Her arms had gone around Breezy's neck. They reached the front door and Jake reached around her to push it open, a small touch of chivalry she hadn't expected.

As they stepped inside, Violet struggled to be free. Breezy let the little girl down and Violet toddled as quickly as her little legs could carry her. In the center of the living room, she looked around, unsure. And then she cried.

"Momma!" Violet wailed, walking through the room. "Momma!"

Jake went after her, scooping her up with his free arm. "It's okay, baby girl."

By then both twins were crying and clinging to Jake.

"I'm sorry." Breezy stood helpless and unsure of how to help. Should she reach for the twins? Maybe she didn't have the mom gene. How could she, really? She'd never truly had a mother of her own.

Jake noticed and his expression softened although the concern remained in his eyes.

"It isn't your fault. It's just too soon to bring them here."

Breezy looked around, trying to come up with something. "They have toys here. Let's pull out the toys and let them settle down. I'm not sure that avoiding this house is what they need. They lived here. It's familiar to them."

"I think I know where they lived."

"I think you should give me a chance." She reached over and this time Rosie held her arms out and fell into Breezy's embrace. The toddler's arms around her neck took her by surprise.

"I'm working on it," he said in a raspy voice.

Of course he was. She sat down on the edge of the sofa and Rose slid off her lap and headed for the guitar Breezy had left leaning against the wall. The little girl moved quickly. Breezy moved faster, getting the instrument before the child could grab it. But she held it, letting Rose pluck the strings. With a few strands of hair on top of her head in a pink bow, Rose smiled and jabbered.

"Do you want a song?" Breezy asked, settling on the sofa again. Rose rested against her knees.

Jake had moved to the nearby chair, still holding Violet. As Breezy started to play, the child slid down from his lap and joined Rose. Breezy swallowed past the lump of emotion that lodged in her throat. She managed not to cry. Instead she sang a Christmas song because it sounded like one a child would be soothed by.

As she sang, Rose clapped a few times and sounded as if she might be singing along. But it was hard to tell in the language of a two-year-old. She finished and set the guitar back on the floor. Violet had wandered back to Jake and was leaning against him, her thumb in her mouth, twirling dark curls around her finger.

He cleared his throat, and the little girl looked up at him. He scooped her into his arms. "We should feed them."

"Yes, of course."

If the music had soothed the girls, it seemed to have had the opposite effect on Jake. He headed off to the kitchen like a lion with a thorn in his paw. She remembered the folk tale, and knew, with certainty, that she wasn't the mouse who would offer to remove the thorn. She wouldn't want to get that close to the lion.

"I made soup and grilled cheese." She walked to the stove, ignoring the man who had taken the girls to the dining room. "I have the sandwiches ready to grill and the soup is warm."

She wasn't about to admit that she'd pondered for a very long time over what to feed the girls. She had no idea if they could eat a sandwich or if they were still eating baby food.

"They'll eat that." He settled Violet in her high chair and then reached for Rosie.

Breezy watched from the doorway but then turned to the kitchen and the job of finishing lunch. She turned the griddle on and pulled the already buttered bread out of the fridge, along with the cheese slices she would put in the middle. When she had them on the electric griddle, she found Jake Martin in the doorway watching her.

"You play well," he said in an easy tone.

"Thank you," she said, turning back to the griddle. "What would you like to drink?"

"I can get our drinks. The girls are buckled in and I can see them from here," he offered as he took glasses from the cabinet.

She nodded, as if she wasn't making a mental list of parenting dos and don'ts. One: always make sure they are buckled and within line of sight. Yes, those things seemed like common sense, but what if she forgot something? What if there was a rule that most people knew but she didn't? She'd learned a lot of those rules when she'd moved in with Mia, but Mia's stepson, Caleb, was almost seven now. He didn't require safety seats or high chairs anymore.

"Are you talking to yourself?" He opened the fridge and pulled out the pitcher of tea she'd made that morning. Tea should never be instant. Mia had taught her that rule. There were other rules, too. Going to church on Sunday was another one.

Had she been talking to herself? She bit down on her bottom lip and shook her head, hoping that was the right answer. "No, of course not. I was telling you there are sippy cups here and milk in the fridge."

"Of course. Because the word *milk* sounds like *rules*."

"It could," she hedged. She flipped the sandwiches off the griddle onto a plate.

He laughed. "You're kidding, right?"

She started to feel a little bubble of laughter coming to the surface. She didn't want to laugh, not with him. Laughing with Jake would make them feel like friends and he clearly was *not* a friend.

"There aren't rules, Breezy."

"Aren't there?"

She ladled the soup into bowls, adding just a tiny amount for the twins. How much soup would they eat?

"A little more than that," Jake responded to her unasked question. "And I guess there *are* some rules."

Great, she loved rules. She might as well ask now and get it over with before she broke them all and found herself dismissed from the lives of her nieces. He'd made it clear he had the power to do that.

"Okay, tell me the rules."

Jake cut up the sandwiches and placed them in front of the girls. She'd forgotten to do that. Next time, sandwiches in four triangles. That was simple enough. She set the soup on the table. Jake moved it back.

"What?"

"Soup out of reach or it'll be on the floor before we can turn around."

"Rule one, no soup."

He laughed, the sound a little rusty but nice. He should laugh more often.

"I didn't say no soup," he clarified. "I said out of reach."

She handed him a glass of tea and he took the seat next to Violet. Breezy took that as her cue and moved to the seat next to Rose. The little girl had already reached for a triangle of sandwich and was nibbling crust.

"Next rule?" Breezy asked as she reached for her sandwich.

Jake held out his hand. "We pray before we eat."

Of course. She let out a sigh and took the hand he offered. She ignored the fact that with one hand in his and one hand holding Rose's, she felt connected.

And a little bit trapped. No, she couldn't ignore that.

Jake took a bite of sandwich and nearly choked. "What in the world is that?"

Next to him Violet gagged. Rose continued to nibble as if it was the best thing she'd ever eaten.

"It's grilled cheese."

"That is *not* cheese," he pointed out.

"No, it's not," she admitted. "It's cheese substitute."

Jake put the sandwich down on his plate and took a long drink of tea, hoping it was real tea. It was. After he washed the taste of fake cheese out of his mouth he pinned the woman across from him with a look. "Rule three, no fake cheese. That's not even real food."

She laughed a little and smiled at Rose, who was happily chowing down. Rose grinned up at Breezy. Drool and cheese slid down her chin.

"Rose likes it," she informed him.

"Rose doesn't know better." He pushed back from the table and headed for the kitchen. "I think we'll have more soup and crackers, if you haven't found a substitute for those."

When he returned to the dining room, she

looked less than sure of herself. "I thought it would be healthier for them."

"They're two, they need to eat dairy." He ladled more soup in the bowls and tossed a sleeve of crackers in front of Breezy. She had taken a bite of sandwich and made a face.

"It is pretty gross."

"So you're not really a vegetarian?"

She shook her head. "No, I just thought it sounded like the right thing for children."

He laughed and then she laughed. Maybe this is how they would get through this mess, with laughter. Maybe they would work out a friendship and he would learn to trust her. But he wasn't ready for that. Not right now. He sat back down and pushed the sandwich away. "I think maybe next time we'll stick to real cheese."

"Right," she said. "And maybe we should go over the rest of the rules."

He leaned back in his chair, his gaze settling on Violet's dark hair as she sipped soup from her spoon. "It isn't as if I've made a list of rules, Breezy. I'm not trying to make this difficult. I just have to be the person who keeps them safe."

"You think you're on your own with this?"

He didn't answer the question because he didn't want to explain that having Sylvia Martin for a mother meant he'd been taking care of children since he'd been old enough to reach the stove.

He didn't know how to let go. And in his experience, women had a tendency not to stick around. At least not the ones in his life.

"I'm not on my own," he finally answered. "But I'm the head of this family and I will always make sure these little girls are taken care of."

"Maybe give me the benefit of the doubt and understand that I want the same for them. I want them happy and healthy. I want to be part of their lives." She leaned a little in his direction. "C'mon. Give me the rules. You know it'll make you feel better."

"I don't know what the rules are." Even as he said it he found himself smiling, and surprised by that. She did that, he realized. She undid his resolve with a cheerful smile and a teasing glint in her golden-brown eyes.

"You have rules," she said. "Should I get some paper or do you think I can remember them all?"

"Okay. Church. We always attend church."

She smiled at that. "Because it's a law in Martin's Crossing or because you are a man of faith?"

"What does that mean?"

She shrugged. "You made it sound like a law," she said. "If broken, they'll what? Stone me in the town square?"

"No, they won't stone you in the town square and yes, I'm a man of faith."

"Okay, Rule Number Three, church. I can do church."

There was a hesitance to her voice that he wanted to question but he didn't.

"We eat as a family on Sunday afternoons."

"Am I considered family now?"

"You're family." He hadn't planned this, for her to be in their lives, a part of their family, but she was. Man, she complicated his life in so many ways.

On the other hand, the rules made him smile, because he'd never intended to list them. He hadn't even thought of them as rules until she pointed it out.

"Okay, church and Sunday dinner. That's nice. What if I bring the tofu pizza?"

"Rule Number Five…"

She laughed. "No tofu?"

"Never." He pushed back from the table and she did the same. "I need to check on the cattle."

"Is checking on cattle a rule?" She grinned at him.

"No, it isn't a rule. It's something that has to be done."

"Can I help you do things here? I mean, I'm going to be around, I might as well earn my keep."

He unbuckled Violet and lifted her from the high chair. He hadn't expected Breezy to offer her help. What was he supposed to tell her, that he'd been looking for an excuse to get away from her for a few minutes? He hadn't expected her to tease, and he definitely hadn't expected to enjoy her company.

"You want to help out with the cattle?"

She looked a little unsure. "Well, maybe. I mean, is there a way I can help?"

"Have you ever lived on a ranch, Breezy?"

"My sister was raised on a ranch in Oklahoma."

"But you, have *you* ever lived on a ranch?"

"I've seen cows." She said it with a wink.

He held Violet close but he smiled at the woman opposite him. "You've seen cows but thought cheese came from a plant?"

"Okay, let's not mention that anymore, and I promise to never buy nondairy again."

"Thank you. I can't even believe they had such a thing at the store in town. And we still have a few rules to cover."

"Such as?" She had Rose in her arms and the little girl's eyes were droopy. Breezy kissed her cheek and stroked her hair, causing those droopy eyes to close and her head to nod. She'd be asleep in a few minutes. So would Violet.

He headed for the living room and she followed. "If you are here long enough to date, we don't bring dates home, or around the girls."

"That's absurd. Are you planning to stay single until they're eighteen?"

He didn't like the question, and as he settled into a rocking chair with Violet he tried to ignore it. Bottom line was he wouldn't let a mother walk out on Violet and Rose. The twins had already lost enough.

Violet nodded off in his arms. Rose was already on the sofa, a blanket pulled up over her. He started to get out of the rocking chair with Violet but Breezy moved to take her from him, her blond hair falling forward. The silky strands brushed his arms as she lifted his niece. Their hands touched and he looked up to meet her gaze head-on.

The strangest feelings erupted as she moved away from him with Violet in her arms. It made him want to reach out to her, to know her better, to trust her.

He shook off those thoughts because they didn't make sense.

He watched as she carried Violet away from him, cradling her gently and then settling her on the opposite end of the sofa from her sister.

He remained in the rocking chair, as she covered the little girl with a pink afghan. She kissed Violet's cheek and brushed her hair back from her face.

If she was going to leave, he hoped she left before the twins got used to her touch, to her softness.

"I'm going to the barn," he said, heading for the front door. She didn't have a chance to question him. He didn't need more tangled-up emotions to deal with. He needed fresh air and a few minutes to clear his thoughts.

And a few rules for himself when it came to Breezy Hernandez.

## Chapter Four

Thursday morning, just a few days into this new life of hers, Breezy stepped outside with a cup of coffee. It was cool, crisp, but not cold. She breathed in the slightly frosty air as she settled in a rocking chair on the front porch. The land stretching forever in front of her was different than Oklahoma, yet similar. The terrain surrounding the house was flat with small trees; the leaves had turned and were falling. An old barn stood in the field, gray wood against a backdrop of a foggy morning. A short distance away the ground rose in rugged hills, also dotted with trees. She knew there was a lake not far from Martin's Crossing, and the creek that ran through this property emptied into that lake.

The sun rose, turning the frosty air to morning fog and touching everything in pinkish-gold. It made her think of faith, of believing in something other than herself. She'd tried, since she was little, to capture that faith.

Not just the faith, but what came with it. The sense of having purpose, of belonging, of Sunday dinners and laughing families.

She wanted that life. She wanted a home that would always be hers, with belongings that were hers. Maybe she wouldn't have to leave. Maybe she could fill this house with pictures and things she collected.

Her gaze drifted in the direction of the metal barn, a newer structure, part lean-to for cattle and part machine shed for farm equipment. Something was off. She tried to figure out what was different. And then she saw the cattle moving outside an open gate.

They definitely shouldn't be out. She would have to do something about the problem.

She set her cup down and slipped her feet into her slippers As she ran across the yard and then down the dirt track to the barn, she was struck with the realization that she didn't have a clue what she needed to do once she reached the cattle. Of course she knew she should put them back in the field. But exactly how did a person go about putting up a small herd of cattle?

As she ran she shouted and waved her arms. The cattle continued to drift, separating into several small groups. They were gigantic black beasts. One eyed her with a glare. She glared back.

"Back inside that gate, you wooly mammoths." She waved her arms and ran at the animals.

For the most part they stood their ground. A few moved out of her way but definitely not toward the gate. Several dropped their heads to graze on winter-brown grass. One took several cautious steps in her direction.

She paused to watch, hopeful he wasn't going to charge her but not really positive. Time for a new tactic.

"Back in the field. If you please, Sir Loin."

She shooed him with her hands. He shook his massive head. She started to run at him, slipping a little on the frosty grass.

"Listen, hamburger, I was giving you the benefit of the doubt when I thought you were a gentleman, now go." She charged at him, waving her arms.

He snorted and took a few quick steps away from her before turning back to face her again. It clicked in her city-girl brain that she wasn't going to win a battle against a one-ton animal. Plus, she had nowhere to run. The small herd of cattle were between her and the barn. The house was a few hundred feet behind her. There were definitely no trees to climb.

Her legs suddenly grew a little shaky and she started to worry how much it would hurt to be trampled by a bull. He had turned his attention back to her. The other cows were grazing and moving away. Maybe she should have started with them because they definitely looked less aggressive.

*Walk away, slow and easy.* It was the same advice she'd given herself on city streets at night when someone walked a little too closely behind her or came out of an alley looking for trouble. Never let them see your fear.

She started to walk, glancing over her shoulder to make sure he wasn't going to charge. He seemed content to watch. But as she moved toward the barn, she heard him moving. She looked back over her shoulder and he was trotting toward her, his head lowered.

"No!" She started to run.

Sharp barks and the sound of a horse's hooves broke through her fear-fogged brain. She saw the flash as a dog rushed past her, heard his warning barks, and then a horse moved next to her. She looked up, her entire body turning to jello as her heart tried to beat itself out of her chest.

Jake Martin smiled down at her and then he

swung, with casual ease, from the saddle. He landed lightly on the ground, all six-plus-feet of him.

"Having some troubles, Miss Hernandez?"

"Oh, no, I just felt like playing with the cattle, Mr. Martin. They seemed lonely. I thought the bull would like to play fetch."

"Yes." He grinned. "Bulls do love to play fetch. I hate to ruin your fun, but what say we put your playmates back in the field and figure out how they got loose."

"Good idea." She peeked around his horse, a red-gold animal that was huge, because a man like Jake Martin needed a huge beast to ride.

The dog, a heeler, was having a great time circling the cattle and bringing them toward the gate.

"Why don't you wait inside the barn?" Jake pointed and she nodded in agreement, her insides settling now that he was there.

He swung back into the saddle and the horse spun in a tight half circle, going after a few cows that were making for the house and the yard. Breezy watched from the door of the barn, somewhat entranced by the beauty of it. Jake's horse seemed to obey with the slightest touch of his hands on the reins or his knees on its sides. The dog kept an eye on the cattle and an ear perked toward Jake, waiting for various commands.

Within minutes the cattle were back in the field and the gate was closed. Jake slid to the ground again and wrapped the reins around a post. The dog plopped down on the ground and proceeded to lick his paws.

Jake walked toward her, no longer smiling but giving the place a careful look. When he got to her, he peeked inside the barn.

"Have you been in there?"

She shook her head. "No. I was sitting on the porch with a cup of coffee when I saw that they were out and this door was open."

"The door was open?" His brows came together and his eyes narrowed. "You haven't been out here at all?"

"No, of course not."

"I'm sorry, I'm not accusing you, just trying to figure things out. Stay out here."

"No!"

He smiled, his features relaxing. "Chicken?"

"No, of course not. But why would I stay out here if you're going in there?"

He pushed the door open a little wider and motioned her inside. "By all means, be my guest."

She stepped inside the hazy, dark interior of the barn. Jake was right behind her, his arm brushing hers as he stepped around her. Without a word he headed down the center aisle for the open door at the other end.

"You haven't seen anyone? Any cars? Any sounds last night?"

"Nothing."

He slowed as he reached the open door. For the first time she felt a sliver of fear. It shivered up her spine as she stepped close to the wall. Jake eased close to the room and looked inside. And then he stepped through that door, leaving her somewhat alone.

"Is everything okay?" she whispered.

He stepped out of the room, shaking his head. "The office is ransacked. I'm not sure what anyone was hoping to find in there. But I'm going to call the police and file a report, just to be on the safe side."

So much for her calm, peaceful existence in Martin's Crossing. Breezy sank with relief onto an overturned bucket and watched as Jake paced a short distance away from her. He spoke quietly on his cell phone, making it impossible to hear him. But she couldn't help wondering if he suspected her. Why wouldn't he? She'd showed up in town, the mysterious sister of Lawton Brooks. She was a woman who had lived on the streets. Her resume included panhandling, singing for change and an arrest record—although no charges were ever filed. Why wouldn't he suspect her? Most people did.

Even her sister Mia's husband, Slade, had been a little on the suspicious side when he first found her. He'd looked into her past and dug up what dirt he could find. He'd done it for Mia. Even bringing her to Oklahoma had been for Mia, not for Breezy.

It had worked out, though. And had given her a taste of what it was like to belong. It had only been a few days, but she wanted to belong in Martin's Crossing. Belong to a town with a small grocery store and neighbors who asked how she was doing.

Jake ended his call and walked back toward her. With his long, powerful strides he was there in a matter of steps. He kneeled next to her, bending those long legs and folding his arms over his knees. He pushed back the black cowboy hat and peered at her. He looked concerned.

She took a breath and waited.

"Are you okay?"

"Of course I am." She made sure to smile as she said it. "Why wouldn't I be?"

His face split in a grin. "Well, you were almost toast out there with Johnny."

"The bull's name is Johnny? How ridiculous."

Eye brows arched. "Really? What would you name him?"

She shook her head. "I thought perhaps Sir Loin. But then he didn't seem very chivalrous for a knight, so maybe Johnny is better."

"He usually isn't aggressive, but he does like to play. And when a bull his size decides to play, that makes you the bouncy ball."

"I'm glad you came along when you did."

"Me, too," he replied. His voice was soft, like wind through the pines, and it undid her a tiny bit. "You're probably cold."

She was cold. She'd been wearing yoga pants and a T-shirt when she'd gone on this wild adventure. And her slippers were soaked from the damp morning grass. As she considered her pathetic condition, he slipped off his jacket and eased it around her shoulders.

"This should help."

Words failed her. The jacket smelled of Jake Martin, like pine, mountains in the fall and cold winter air. She wanted to bury her nose in the collar and inhale his scent. She wanted to tell him she didn't need his jacket. Without his jacket she was safe. Not tangled up with him, longing to be a part of something she'd never be a part of. In her experience, wanting always ended with disappointment. What she wanted was always taken from her or left behind when she moved on.

\* \* \*

Jake watched as a train of emotions flickered across her face. He'd seen gratitude when he'd first put that coat around her, then he'd seen fear and maybe regret. He wished she wasn't so easy to read. She'd be less complicated if she could be as composed as she thought she was.

Breezy was poetry, classic novels and maybe the Bible, all rolled into one very open book. It was a book he thought he might like to read. In any other life but his own.

For Violet and Rose's sakes, he couldn't mess this up. He'd seen, even in their short introduction to Breezy, that the girls would need this woman in their lives. But he couldn't need her. His entire life was a juggling act. The ranch, his career, the twins, his family. One more thing might set the whole mess falling fast around him.

But he would handle the moments when she made him smile, made him laugh. He was selfish that way.

"Do you want to go back to the house?" he asked, needing to get past whatever vibrated in the air between them.

She shook her head; he'd known she would. "I'm cold, but I'm not going to faint or fall apart, Martin."

He smiled again. "I didn't begin to think you would, Hernandez."

At that she actually smiled, and he saw her vulnerability slip away. She was strong again. Snuggled in his jacket that she would leave scented with her lavender-and-citrus fragrance.

"If you need to do something, go right ahead," she offered. "I know you didn't come over here with the intention of rescuing me and then solving a mystery."

"No, I came over to feed. To do that, I'll have to get the tractor and hook a round bale. I'll be gone in about fifteen minutes."

"I haven't forgotten how to protect myself. I've been doing it a long time."

He had no doubt she could protect herself. And he also knew that was her way of telling him she didn't need him to look after her. He walked away, taking a spare jacket that had been left inside the tack room and heading out the side door to the tractor. He climbed up into the big green-and-yellow machine and closed the door, blocking out the sounds and thoughts that were bombarding him this morning.

But one thought wouldn't be evaded. When was the last time anyone had looked out for Breezy? Had she ever been made to feel safe, to feel protected?

It wasn't his job, that role of protector. She did have a sister in Oklahoma. And she had made it clear that she relied on herself, her own abilities.

Jake had the twins, Samantha, Brody and sometimes Duke to watch over, to keep out of trouble and to protect. Lawton had put Breezy in his life but he hadn't made Jake her guardian.

With that settled in his mind, he drove out through the field with a round bale on the back of the tractor and cattle following behind him. He'd hired a kid to do this job but it hadn't worked out. James had been twenty-one and wanting to save up to go to welding school. After a week of taking care of things at Lawton's place, James had stopped showing up.

That left it to Jake. Maybe when Brody came home he'd help out. And Duke would do what he could.

As he headed back to the barn to park the tractor the county deputy was pulling up in his car. Mac the blue heeler greeted him, his stub tail wagging. Jake knew the deputy. They'd gone to school together a long time ago.

When he stepped back into the barn after parking the tractor, Deputy Aaron Mallard was in the office. Breezy stood in the doorway answering questions and apologizing because she really hadn't seen anything other than loose cattle and an open door.

The deputy nodded in greeting when he saw Jake. "Jake, been a while."

"Aaron, yeah, it has. I didn't touch anything, but I can tell you it wasn't like this yesterday."

"Didn't figure you left it a mess. And I know Lawton was a stickler for neatness. Someone was looking for something in the filing cabinet. It's pried open. Funny, because I'm not seeing anything but feed bills and farm equipment receipts."

"That's really all that we kept in here."

"Anything in the house that someone would want?"

"I guess there could still be paperwork or research in Lawton's office. He took most of his work to Austin but sometimes he worked at home," Jake responded. He tried to remember anything Lawton had said or even hinted at. Had they had prowlers before? It wasn't unheard-of these days.

The country used to be safe. They hadn't locked their doors for more years than he could remember. Yeah, life had changed. People didn't mind stealing from neighbors. Worse than that, now they even stole from the church if they got a chance.

What had happened to respect? Leaning against the door frame, he shook his head at the turn of his thoughts. "I'll take a look around, and see if I can find anything that might have been interesting to a burglar."

"Could be it isn't a burglar, Jake." The deputy closed the filing cabinet drawer and walked out of the office. "Could be they're searching for something and it isn't a random break-in. Lawton developed some pretty serious financial software. Could he have left something around here that he was working on? Something new?"

"Yeah, maybe," Jake agreed, trying hard not to think about how this put the twins, and Breezy, in danger. If someone was searching for Lawton's latest project, what would they do to get their hands on it?

"I'll make sure we send a patrol by here a couple of times a day, and you all keep the alarm system activated." The deputy gave Breezy a look this time. "And keep the doors locked."

Jake walked Aaron out. They discussed the odds of it being someone they knew. They talked about the weather and Christmas. As they talked, Breezy walked out of the barn, closing the door behind her. She told Jake she'd meet him at the house.

She was still wearing his jacket. He watched her walk down the driveway, his dog next to her. He knew her scent would linger on his jacket. Every time he pulled it on, he'd smell that light spring fragrance.

Jake had been around awhile. He knew temptation when he saw it, when it walked away with his dog and his coat. And maybe took a little of his common sense with it.

It had been years since he'd met temptation head-on like this, but he still recognized it for what it was. And he still knew where that road led. He knew he wasn't going there.

## Chapter Five

After Jake left, Breezy decided to unpack her few belongings. She'd been putting off the task of settling in, thinking something would happen, preparing for the reality that this, too, could be taken from her. She'd kept her clothes in her suitcase and her toiletries in the bag she'd put on the bathroom counter. Unpacking meant staying. Unpacking meant a commitment to remain here and help raise two little girls.

It meant staying in Jake Martin's life. For a long, long time. Always being the person he tolerated. A person he'd rather not have in his world.

She had news for him. He was no picnic, either. But they were stuck with each other and she'd make the best of it.

The decision to stay meant picking a room. There were two bedrooms and a craft room upstairs. She had picked a spare room on the ground floor, close to the room that had belonged to the twins. A room those twins would return to in time. They would spend nights with her. Maybe even weeks.

Breezy's new room was pretty with tan, textured walls and another wall of stone, with a fireplace in the center and French doors that led to a patio. She stood in the middle of that room and tried to imagine herself living there. She tried to picture herself helping Jake Martin raise two little girls, picture them growing up. She would be there as they went to school, as they started to think about boys and dating, and then someday they would leave. And where would she be then? Still in Martin's Crossing, still single and wishing she could find a place to belong?

What if she grew to love this town?

How would it feel to grow old in Martin's Crossing? For some reason, images of Jake Martin popped into her mind. Unattainable, undeniably gorgeous, a man with rules, a man of faith. She would be coparenting those little girls with a man who was everything she'd never been.

She headed down the hall to the kitchen, where she quickly made a list of things she needed from the store. What she really needed was to get out of the house. Breezy headed for

Martin's Crossing, AKA: The One-Horse Town. As she drove she called Mia. She needed to tell her sister everything that had happened. She also needed to know she still had an ally, someone who trusted her.

"Hey, sis." Mia sounded bright, happy. Of course she was happy; she'd found the man of her dreams in Slade McKennon and the two of them were having a baby. "How are you?"

"I'm good. It looks as if I'll be staying here awhile."

"Really? But…"

"Lawton left me something in his will." Her voice choked as she said it, and she blinked away the threat of tears.

"Breezy, are you okay? Do you need me to come down?"

Breezy cleared her throat. "I'm good. Mia, he left me joint custody of his little girls."

"Girls. As in children?"

"Twins. They're toddlers." She paused, because saying it would make it real. "I'm going to have to stay here."

"Oh, Breezy, no. You were just getting settled. You still have your things at my house."

A few things in boxes she'd never unpacked. Even at Mia's she'd had a hard time believing she had a place to stay. And there wasn't much in those boxes. A few stray seashells, a photograph of herself singing at a coffee shop in Pasadena and a Christmas ornament. Because families had Christmas ornaments they kept and hung up each year. She'd bought one for her tree at Mia's.

"I'll be able to come up eventually. But for now, I'm going to have to stay close to Martin's Crossing."

"Are you sure you're okay?" Mia, a former federal agent, couldn't let go of that instinct to look beneath the surface. Breezy smiled, thankful, so thankful, for her sister. They'd spent almost twenty years apart but they'd been busy reconnecting, making up for that lost time.

"I'm really okay. I've been in worse places." Homeless shelters, on the street, alone.

"I'll be praying for you."

Mia's words came so easily. Her life with the Coopers had been grounded in faith. She had a foundation, one that included a loving and stable family. Breezy's path had been different. She hesitated to answer and Mia knew.

"Breezy, it gets easier."

Believing, having faith, trusting. Yes, she was sure it would get easier. "I know. I'm going to work through this, Mia."

"I know you will. So tell me about the girls."

She smiled. "They're beautiful. They're two

and almost identical. They have dark hair and blue eyes."

A long pause. "And who are you sharing this guardianship with?"

"Lawton's brother-in-law, Jake Martin."

"Oh."

Breezy smiled a little. "Don't say it like that. He's horrible, an absolutely straitlaced grouch."

"And there's nothing worse than straitlaced grouches, right?" Mia teased. "Who, other than you, calls a man 'straitlaced'? Does he wear cardigans with elbow patches, maybe he has thick glasses and…"

Breezy laughed at the image. "Stop! He's just… Well, he has rules."

Their discussion of Jake unfortunately brought an image of the man to mind, and it sure wasn't straitlaced. He was a man who made a girl dream of chivalry, of being rescued, of being protected. She'd never counted on being rescued, and she'd learned at an early age that she could only count on herself.

For years Mia had been on the list of people she didn't count on. As a little girl, Breezy had spent several years waiting for her sister to find her, to rescue her. Because as children it was Mia who looked out for her. Mia had made sure she didn't go hungry. But Mia hadn't shown up and Breezy, the child, hadn't understood that her sister had been a child, too.

"Shudder! A man with rules," Mia said, bringing her back to the conversation.

"You're not helping."

"No," Mia agreed, "I'm not. I'm sure he's perfectly horrible. I think I'll look up Jake Martin of Martin's Crossing on Google and see what I come up with."

"Please don't." Because she knew that would only convince Mia to begin plotting Breezy's demise. Or marriage. "Just say your prayers for me and I'll keep you posted."

"I love you, Breeze," Mia said. The words, even spoken from so far away, made all the difference.

"Love you, too."

Breezy ended the call as she drove past the city-limit sign of Martin's Crossing, population 678. She wasn't quite to town. There were a few farmhouses with barns scattered about, and a flea market with a gravel parking lot a little farther in. The building that housed the flea market was decorated for Christmas with lights wrapped around the posts, and plastic deer with red bows on their necks placed along the exterior. A tree, big and tacky, had been decorated with garland and big ornaments.

Ahead of her she could see the gas station on

the left. On the right was the Martin's Crossing Community Church and fellowship hall. Next to it was a large open area and a park. A block down from the church she knew would be a left-hand turn that was the main street of Martin's Crossing. A street that was wide, and had a couple of businesses on either side. She'd noticed a restaurant called Duke's No Bar and Grill, just down from it was the feed store and across from that was the grocery and a tiny gift and clothing store. She had seen a couple of other businesses that she would check out in time.

Welcome to Martin's Crossing.

She pulled into a parking space in front of the grocery store and got out. In front of her a man had just opened a ladder and was climbing up it, holding a string of lights. The building in front of him was tiny and narrow, with a single door and a window. The sign on the window claimed it to be the home of the wood-carved nativity. Above that sign was one that heralded the name of the building as Lefty's Arts and Antiques.

"Hey there, young lady." He smiled down at her.

"Hello."

"You must be Lawton's sister."

Breezy was surprised. "How did you know?"

He grinned. "Word travels fast in a town like Martin's Crossing."

"Yes, I'm sure it does."

"Could you hand me up the string of lights and hold them as I hook them up to this overhang?" He grinned down at her again. He had white hair, gray eyes and a smile that took away her reservations, that part of her that always held back.

"Of course." She held up the lights and he pulled a hammer out of the tool belt hanging from his waist.

"Thank you. My name's Lefty. Lefty Mueller. I've been in this town all of my life."

"I see," she said, not knowing what else to say. His gray brows drew together as he squinted, watching her with equally gray eyes.

"And your name is…?" he asked as he raised his arms to hook lights along the overhang.

"Oh, I'm sorry. I'm Breezy Hernandez."

"Lovely, very lovely. Well, I'm glad you've come to Martin's Crossing, Breezy Hernandez." He grinned. "We can always use a fresh breeze."

She smiled at the turn of phrase. "You're very charming."

"I do my best." He slipped lights over another hook. "And I love to think that I help bring Christmas cheer to this little town. I've got these lights now. You go on inside and look around."

She glanced toward the grocery store, wondering what time it closed, then gave up and walked through the door of Lefty's little shop. As she stepped inside a Christmas carol played, ending abruptly when the door latched. The interior of the store made it easy to believe that Christmas was less than four weeks away.

The tiny shop was a maze of tables filled with all types of nativities. A nativity mobile hung from the ceiling in the center of the room and another nativity lit with candles spun in a slow circle on the counter. Breezy stopped in front of one that had the tiniest baby Jesus, his minuscule hands reaching for his mother as Joseph looked over Mary's shoulder with obvious pride. A music box attached to the side had a switch and she flipped it. "Away in a Manger" played in soft, music-box tones and the angel on top of the manger spun with wings spread.

The door opened. She turned, smiling at the creator of this art that she never would have imagined in a town like Martin's Crossing.

"Do you like it?" Lefty stepped close, settling a pair of wire-framed glasses on his rather large nose.

"They're all beautiful," she answered.

"This one is yours." He indicated the one she'd been looking at.

"No, I can't. I mean…"

He smiled back at her. "Breezy, you should have a nativity. Do you have one?"

She'd never had one in her life. She'd seen them in front of churches, sometimes home-made, sometimes made from brightly colored plastic. She had loved the one that Mia's family put up in their home each year. But she'd never had one of her own. She didn't want to think about all of the things she hadn't had because they'd moved so often. She'd had a few dolls, but each time they moved on the dolls were left behind. The books were left. Friends were left. She'd learned early that getting attached hurt.

It had become easier to not have, to not get attached. Lefty Mueller stood behind the counter, staring at her over the frames of his glasses. She managed a smile and he nodded, as if that meant acceptance.

"It's yours, so don't argue. It's my welcome gift to you. You see, my great grandfather was German. He settled here, where he continued to do his wood carvings, and he taught his son, who taught his son. What good is such a gift if it can't be shared with people we meet?"

"But you can't just give it to me. I can buy it."

"Then it wouldn't be a gift, my friend. It wouldn't be a story you can share someday, about an old man who shared a piece of Christ-mas with you."

As he'd been talking, he had been wrapping

the nativity in paper and then settling the pieces in a box.

"Thank you." She spoke softly, afraid she would cry at his kindness.

"You're very welcome. Someday you will tell stories about this nativity. Let them be stories of faith, of an old man who carved what he knew best, a savior."

She nodded as he handed her the box. He came out from behind the counter and she gave him a quick hug. He chuckled as he hugged her back.

"I will treasure it forever, Lefty."

"And I hope you find the meaning of it all, Breezy."

"Yes, of course."

He opened the door for her and she walked out, putting the nativity in the front seat of her car. Across the street, a car door slammed. She looked that way and saw Jake Martin. Of course it was. He would be everywhere in this small town. He waved, then proceeded to pull a pine tree from the bed of his truck. He wore gloves and a long-sleeved shirt. His hat was pulled low.

She turned away from him and bumped into a man coming down the sidewalk. He steadied her but then moved back. Breezy studied the elderly man with an oversize coat, dusty, bent-up hat and several days' growth of whiskers on his craggy face.

"I'm so sorry," she said quickly.

"No need to apologize, miss. I wasn't really watching where I was going, either." He grinned a little, holding tight to a potted poinsettia. "But I wasn't watching Jake Martin, either."

"Oh, I…"

"No need," he said. "I would guess you're the aunt of those two little girls."

"I am." Did *everyone* in town know her business? She didn't even know this man's name. "And you are?"

"Joe, I'm Joe."

"You live here in Martin's Crossing?"

His smile shifted and she saw sadness in his eyes. "Oh, I guess I do. I'm passing through, eventually. But it seemed a good place to spend Christmas."

"Yes, it does seem like it would be." She studied his face, his eyes, and she thought she understood Joe.

"Let me offer you this lovely welcoming gift." Joe held out the plant with its bright red flowers.

"But I…I couldn't take your poinsettia."

"Nonsense." He smiled and pushed the potted plant at her, settling it in her hands. "I've nowhere really to keep it and there's nothing better than a poinsettia to put a person in the holiday mood."

"But it's yours."

"Now it belongs to you."

And with a tip of his dirty, bent-up hat, he left. Breezy watched him walk down the street. Then she put the poinsettia in her car, setting it next to the nativity. After locking the car door she looked in the direction Joe had gone, but he'd already vanished from sight. She headed for the grocery store.

The Martin's Crossing grocer had hardwood floors, three aisles and a meat counter in the back next to produce that was labeled Locally Grown and Worth It.

A woman came out from the back of the store through swinging doors, wiping her hands on an apron that hung from her waist. She was middle-aged with short brown hair and an open smile.

"Well, hello."

Breezy smiled as she filled a basket with fruit. "Hello."

The woman followed her down the cereal aisle. "I'm Wanda Howard. My husband, Gene, and I own this place. And you must be Lawton's sister."

"Yes, I am." She smiled and held out a hand.

"I'm Breezy Hernandez. I believe I met your husband the other day."

"Yes, you did. And we're looking forward to having you with us at church on Sunday."

"Yes, of course."

Because that's what a person did when she lived in a small town where everyone knew her name—she went to church. That person would also have a plant and even a nativity to set out for Christmas each year.

As she walked back to her car with her bags of groceries, she saw Jake on the long, covered porch of Duke's. He wore faded jeans, work boots and a shirt with the sleeves rolled to his elbows. She thought that a person who lived in Martin's Crossing would also manage to be friends with Jake Martin.

Friendship was easy.

And then she thought of his many rules and she added one for herself. *Rule Number Five: don't lie to yourself.*

Jake unloaded the tub of decorations for his brother Duke and headed across the street to the grocery store to have a talk with Miss Breezy Hernandez.

"Where are you going?" Duke called out from the door of his restaurant.

Jake glanced back at his brother. "I need a word with Breezy."

"You could..."

Jake kept walking. He didn't need Duke's advice. Duke had always found it a little easier to smile, to joke. Duke hadn't been the oldest. He hadn't been the one begging their mother not to pack her bags. Duke hadn't been the one holding Samantha, just a toddler, as their mother drove away. Or trying to keep Brody from chasing her car.

That memory was the one that always undid him.

He raised a hand as he headed across the street, silencing his brother who continued to call out to him. Breezy had come out of the store carrying two bags of groceries. He watched her heft those bags and he couldn't help but smile. He hoped she wasn't buying more fake cheese. Or something as un-Texas as veggie burgers.

The wind whipped her pale blue skirt, wrapping the cotton material around Western boots. She wore a denim jacket and her hair was pulled back in a ponytail. She saw him and smiled.

It made his step falter a little. It took some of the steam out of him and made him forget what he'd been so determined to tell her. He didn't know how she did that because it didn't happen often, that someone sidetracked him.

"Mr. Martin."

"Jake," he corrected.

"Of course, Jake."

He took one of the bags of groceries and followed her to the little economy car she drove. "There's a truck in the garage at Lawton's. You can drive it."

"I'm okay with my car."

He waited as she opened the door and then he set the bag inside, next to a package from Lefty's and the poinsettia he'd seen her accept from Joe.

After she'd closed the car door and stood facing him, he cleared his throat and remembered that he'd approached her for a reason and it had nothing to do with carrying groceries, the lavender scent of her hair or the way she studied him with eyes the color of caramel.

"I saw you with Joe."

"Oh, yes. He gave me a poinsettia."

"You need to be more careful," he started, but stopped when her eyes narrowed to a glare. "I mean, you are going to be a parent. You'll have the girls to think about."

"You're telling me who I can and can't talk to?"

"I'm asking you to be careful with someone you don't know," he explained.

Her smile lit up her eyes. "I don't really know you."

"You're being purposely difficult."

She laughed. "Yes, I am. Are you being purposely bossy?"

No, he was being derailed, sidetracked and maybe even a little convicted for what he'd said about Joe. "I'm not bossy, I'm careful."

"I'm a black belt. I'm very capable of taking care of myself. And that man, Joe, only wanted to do something nice for a stranger. Everyone has been kind today. Lefty gave me a nativity. Mrs. Howard gave me a basket of fruit."

"Joe isn't from Martin's Crossing. We don't know anything about him."

"Do I need to remind you that you don't know anything about me?"

He could have disagreed. But disagreeing would have meant admitting to the private investigator he'd hired when he'd first learned of the will. He should tell her about it. Marty had told him that if they were going to raise the twins together, they needed to be honest and trust each other.

"I don't know everything about you, Breezy. But what I'm learning is that you're too trusting."

"I'm not that trusting. And I'm not afraid of

Joe. I've been Joe. I know what it's like to be on the streets. If you're worried about Joe, you should be worried about me."

"I'm not worried about you." He glanced toward Duke's. This wasn't getting them anywhere. "Let's get a cup of coffee."

She stood there, wind whipping that blue skirt around her legs. She held her hair back with her hand and smiled at him as he made the offer. They had to start somewhere.

Because, like it or not, they were in each other's lives. Lawton and Elizabeth had tied them together, two unlikely people raising two little girls. When Lawton had mentioned it, Jake had tried to talk him out of it. There were better people than him. And Breezy, she was just an unknown.

Lawton had asked him who would be better. They had no one else they would trust the way they trusted Jake. Breezy, they'd told him, would help him get through.

It shouldn't have been like this. It should never have happened at all.

"I don't drink coffee." She paused, studying his face. "But tea would be good."

Jake walked with her across the street, aware that anyone who happened to be in town would be watching the two of them. He'd really stepped in a mess this time. And all because of Joe.

Joe was a man who had done odd jobs around town, been to church a few times, and really hadn't done more than appear to be suspicious. Because no one knew where he'd come from, where he was staying or when he'd be moving on.

They walked up the steps of Duke's. The building was wood-sided, rustic with a long covered porch. In good weather Duke put tables and chairs on that porch for people who wanted to eat outside. This wasn't exactly good weather. The tables were gone and Duke was decorating for Christmas.

The holidays and life would go on. Without Elizabeth and Lawton. They would all continue to live each day. They would raise the twins. They would be happy. They would laugh again, tell jokes and move on with their lives.

All of that made Jake real friendly with the punching bag his dad had strung up in the barn years ago. It gave him something to take his anger out on. Even way back when his mom had walked out on them. She'd left without looking back, occasionally sending a letter to let them know how happy she was in whatever state she lived in.

He'd used that punching bag when he'd caught his ex-fiancée, Alison, cheating on him two months before their wedding. He'd used it when he'd caught Samantha with a hired hand, not doing anything too serious, but serious enough Jake had wanted to hurt the younger man.

He'd used the punching bag a lot the past couple of weeks as grief had torn him up inside. But the woman standing next to him didn't need to know that. He reached past her to open the door and she said a soft "Thank you."

It was midafternoon and there were few customers in Duke's this time of day. Even though the sign said to wait to be seated, he motioned her to a booth on the far wall. He waved at John Gordon, owner of the garage next to the gas station.

"Jake, did you get that backhoe going the other day?" John asked.

"Sure did, John. But I'll probably still bring it in."

John nodded his head and gave both him and Breezy a careful look before returning to the piece of pie on his plate.

As they sat down, the doors to the kitchen opened. Duke walked out, a giant with a goatee, shaved head and big grin.

"Hey, brother, did you decide to come back and help?"

"Brother?" Breezy repeated.

"That's me. Little brother of Jake." Duke

grinned and pulled a chair from a nearby table to sit at the end of their booth. "And you must be Breezy Hernandez?"

"That's me." She smiled at Duke, and Jake didn't know what to make of that. How in the world did Duke, who looked like he brawled behind buildings, put everyone at ease?

"My big brother isn't being too hard to get along with, is he?" Duke said it with a grin directed at Jake, for which Jake wasn't too thankful.

"No, of course not."

"That's good to know."

Jake turned over the coffee cup that was on the table, settling it in the saucer. Maybe Duke would take the hint.

Instead Duke, younger by two years, stretched and settled in. Relaxed. Jake hadn't known many moments in his life like that, when he could let go and pretend everything would get done, everyone would be taken care of.

"You're going to help me put those lights up, right?" Duke gave Jake a kick in the shin. He managed to not flinch.

"Yes, I'm going to help. I dragged them to town for you, didn't I?"

"Yes, you did." Duke continued to study Breezy. "We're kind of big on Christmas here in Martin's Crossing," he explained. "It won't be easy this year but we'll all be together."

Including Breezy, if she stayed. Family now included her. Jake knew it hadn't been Lawton's intention to make him feel responsible for her, but that's the way it worked.

"Christmas is a good time for healing." Duke's voice was low, sending a strong hint. "I think what we all need is a deep breath and something to help us focus a little."

Right, Jake thought, because it was that easy. To forget a sister, a best friend and that the twins had lost their parents.

Duke nailed him with a look. "It isn't going to be easy," Duke responded to Jake's unspoken thoughts. "But we'll get through the way we always do. We're family."

"Yes, family." Jake moved his empty coffee cup. "Do you have a waitress who could pour a cup of coffee and get Breezy a glass of tea?"

"When did you get so impatient?" Duke grinned as he eased out of the chair, unbending his six feet eight inches of solid muscle to tower over them. Jake was only a few inches shorter than his mammoth brother, but even he was a little intimidated. He looked up, smiling at his little brother, as he liked to think of Duke.

"Oh, are you the waitress?" Jake asked. "You need a little cap, or an apron, I think."

Duke's eyes narrowed and he growled a little. "You're asking for it, brother."

As Duke walked away, Jake made eye contact with the woman sitting across from him. She drummed her fingers a little on the table and he wondered what in the world he'd done now.

"So, Christmas with the family. Rule Number Six. Or is it Seven?"

"Are you really going to keep track?"

"It seems like the easiest way to stay out of trouble. Church. Check. No scary vagrants. Check. Real cheese. Check."

He added, "Christmas with the family. Check."

"Gotcha."

"You don't like Christmas?"

"I do. I'm just…"

He waited for her to explain. Duke returned with the coffeepot and a glass of tea. "Pie?"

"Might as well. What do you have?" Jake asked as he reached for the creamer. "Homemade chocolate?"

"Made it myself." He stood there for a moment looking from Jake to Breezy, then back again. He grinned a little too big. "I'll get you a piece and then I guess I'll make myself scarce."

"Sounds like a good idea," Jake agreed.

Duke disappeared through the door to the kitchen. Jake's gaze connected with Breezy's, and he wondered a little more about her past.

He wanted more than the sterile facts uncovered by the private investigator. For a brief moment he saw shades of vulnerability in her eyes and then, quickly, the look was gone. She didn't like to be vulnerable. She was all about being independent. She was about being in control. Yeah, he got her.

But understanding her was the last thing he wanted or needed. What he'd like most would be for her to decide Martin's Crossing was the last place she wanted to be, tied down to him and two little girls. He had a feeling that she wasn't a quitter. He needed to adjust because she was in his life. For better or worse.

## Chapter Six

By Friday Breezy was starting to get a routine going. She'd spent the morning with the twins while Jake worked. After they'd left she'd baked some halfway-decent bread. She was teaching herself to cook. People who lived in one place baked. And cooked. Probably from recipes handed down from generation to generation.

She wanted those recipes. She'd searched through the kitchen hoping to find a book with things like "Grandma's Vegetable Soup," or "Aunt Iva's Homemade Rolls." So far she'd only found a few cookbooks.

If she was going to continue her cooking adventures, she needed more ingredients. Late in the afternoon she cleaned up the kitchen and grabbed her purse. She would head to town, do some shopping and maybe treat herself to dinner at Duke's. She liked Jake's younger brother. He was uncomplicated and easy to talk to.

He didn't make her feel like she should leave. Or make her want to run far and fast.

She parked in front of Oregon's All Things shop. It had been closed for a few days but today it was open. Breezy grabbed her purse and headed toward the front door. As she did, she saw Joe a short distance away. He waved a gloved hand and she waved back, forgetting all about Jake's silly rules.

The bell over the door clanged as she entered Oregon's. The shop was small and cozy. It smelled like freshly baked apple pie, compliments of a candle burning on the counter. There was a row of skirts and tops on one wall. On the adjoining wall were shelves of handmade Christmas ornaments. She noticed one that was hand-painted with a picture of the manger scene. In tiny writing was the author's signature: Oregon.

The door at the back of the shop opened and a woman stepped out. She was small with dark hair and dark eyes. Her smile, when she saw Breezy, was sweet and welcoming.

"Hello, I'm sorry it took me so long to get out here. I had to wash paint off my hands." The woman held out a hand, still slightly damp.

Breezy took it in hers. "I'm Oregon Jeffries. And you must be Breezy."

"I'm beginning to wonder if there's a neon sign over my head," Breezy lamented as she moved from ornaments to clothing, all with the tags stating they were original designs by Oregon.

Oregon laughed. "There is. It flashes your name and the word *newcomer*. Don't worry, the novelty will wear off and then you'll just be one of the folks that lives in Martin's Crossing."

"I'm looking forward to that," she said. She looked around, amazed. "You do all of this?"

Oregon's cheeks turned pink. "I do. I've been sewing my whole life, and painting. It seemed like the best way to keep myself out of trouble."

"I've never sewn." She would add that to her list of things a person staying in one place should do. "I took a sculpting class once, years ago."

"Maybe you'll take it up again?"

Breezy shook her head. "No, I think it was a passing phase. But you, on the other hand, have a gift."

"Sewing and art were my escape from reality," Oregon explained. "My mom moved us around a lot. She had a hobby. Marriage."

"I really understand the moving part."

Oregon smiled. "Yeah, I think you probably do."

Breezy turned back to the Christmas ornaments. She picked one with an angel and a Bible verse and the one with the manger scene. She would add these to her meager collection today. Ornaments she would keep, that she wouldn't have to leave behind.

"I'll take these two."

"Perfect. I'll wrap them for you." Oregon walked behind the counter with the two ornaments. "Are you going to join us tonight at the church? We're decorating the park and the church for the annual Christmas bazaar and the community festival."

"I'm not sure. I didn't know if..." What should she say? That she didn't know if she was included? She wasn't a member. Didn't she need to be a member or a real citizen of Martin's Crossing?

"If?" Oregon asked as she wrapped the decorations. "If you're invited? Of course you are. This is a community event and I've heard it's a lot of fun. They decorate, practice for the community caroling and then have a potluck. There are probably five churches in the area and they'll be working on floats for the parade. The fire station has one, too."

Before Breezy could respond, a girl of about

twelve ran in from the back room. She had dark hair and blue eyes. She looked from Breezy to Oregon.

"Did you finish cleaning for Mrs. Walters?" Oregon asked her.

"I did. And she said to remind you to bring that vegetable thing that you make. And now I'm going over to Duke's. He said if I'll sweep the porch, he'll pay me."

Oregon's smile faded. "When did you make that deal?"

"Last week. Come on, Mom. You said if I want a horse, I have to raise the money and pay for it myself."

"Right, of course, but…" Oregon turned to the register, pushing a few buttons and then handing Breezy a receipt. "But I didn't know you were going to be all over town."

"I'm not all over town. And I am twelve."

"Right, you're twelve. Okay, go sweep, Lilly, but don't be a nuisance."

"Love you, Mom." And out the door the child went.

"She's beautiful," Breezy commented as she pulled out her money.

"And a handful. We've only lived here for six months but she's managed to involve herself in every aspect of the community. She wants to barrel race now. I've tried to tell her it isn't cheap."

"She seems willing to work for it."

"Yes, she does," Oregon answered a little wearily. "So I'll see you in an hour?"

"An hour?"

"At the Community Church."

"Oh, right." Breezy picked up her ornaments. "I'll be there."

An hour later, Breezy walked up to the Community Church. From the sidelines she watched as lights were strung from pole to pole on the outside of the building. The nativity, a homemade affair with a shingle roof, barn-wood sides and carved wooden figures, was the center of everything. Behind it was an outline of an ancient city in glittering white lights.

Inside the stable Joseph and Mary kneeled behind a manger. The display was large enough that real animals would be brought in the night of the Christmas festival. They would have a parade that night and the churches in the area would join together for caroling.

A week before that community event, there was a craft bazaar that brought people from other communities to shop in Martin's Crossing.

Breezy watched all the activity, unsure of where she fit. People were stringing lights in obvious holiday shapes. These people belonged. To Martin's Crossing, to the church and to each other. She considered quietly slipping away. Because she didn't belong.

That was ridiculous and she knew it. She'd always been able to make herself a part of things, to blend in. She'd done it in Dawson, as Mia's sister and as an honorary Cooper. She could do it here. And deep down it meant more to be a part of this town, these people.

A movement to her side stopped the melancholy thoughts. She turned, spotting old Joe. He nodded a greeting as he stepped closer.

"This is the way it should be celebrated," he said with a sad smile.

"I'm sorry?"

He glanced at her, and then looked away. "Christmas. It should be about community. People reaching out to each other."

"Yes, it is nice. I've always thought it should be like this, too." For her, though, it had always been another day.

No, that wasn't true. It had been different. Even for her. It had often been a day when they might have lined up at a soup kitchen or gone to a shelter where gifts were handed out to children.

"It wasn't like this for you?" Joe asked, buttoning the top button of his canvas jacket.

"No, not really. Last year I spent Christmas with my sister. And that was a lot like this."

"Come inside and get cocoa." Joe pointed toward the church fellowship building. "And food. Fill up a plate, get warm and then I bet they'll find a job for you. Pastor Allen is a decent man and you'll enjoy this congregation."

She thanked him for the invitation and allowed him to lead her inside the metal-sided building next to the church. The sign over the door said Community Church Family Center. As they entered, most people smiled. A few were obviously curious about the newcomer and Joe.

She turned her attention back to her escort. "Have you eaten, Joe?"

"I have. And you don't need to worry about me, Miss Hernandez. I'm taking good care of myself."

Of course he was. But was he warm? Did he have a roof over his head at night? She wanted to ask but wasn't sure how. He let her off the hook with an easy, unconcerned look.

"Get yourself that cup of cocoa and some dinner," Joe encouraged, and then he was gone. He was her only friend, it seemed, as she stood there with no one to talk to, no one who knew her.

She was rescued by a familiar giggle. Rose headed her way, toddling on chubby two-year-old legs. She had a doll in one arm and a smudge of chocolate on her cheek.

"Brees." Rosie growled the toddler version of Breezy's name.

"Yes, Brees." She picked the little girl up, holding her close and quickly changed her mind about closeness. "And you do not smell good, little girl."

"Poop." Rosie cackled as she said it, like it was the best news ever.

So what in the world was she supposed to do with a messy little girl? She looked around, wondering where the diaper bag might be. She spotted Jake heading her way, Violet in his arms. He grinned and her heart tumbled a little. The stink no longer mattered, not really. Not when Jake Martin smiled. Truly smiled.

"I see you found my runaway," he said as he settled Violet on his shoulders. "I told her she needs her diaper changed."

"Yes, I kind of noticed. If you have the diaper bag somewhere, I can do it."

"Gladly." He pointed to a table in the corner. "And I'll owe you one."

She was okay with that. The idea of him owing her was suddenly very appealing. "Where should I change her?"

"The nursery is through that door." He pointed. "But I'll show you."

They were almost to the nursery when they were stopped by a woman with light gray hair and pretty brown eyes. She wore jeans and a sweatshirt but she had class that couldn't be denied.

"Jake, this must but Breezy." The woman held a handful of lights but switched them to the other hand and held out her right hand to Breezy.

"Yes." Jake leaned in to kiss the woman's cheek. "Breezy, this is my aunt Patty."

Breezy had to switch Rosie to her other arm to free her hand. Rosie wasn't cooperative. She wanted down.

The woman patted her arm. "No, don't worry. I think you have your hands full."

"She is a handful," Breezy agreed. "And she needs a diaper changed."

"I'll let you go, then. And make sure you get something to eat." Patty started to walk away but stopped and turned to Jake. "Did you hear about the anonymous donation to the church? To buy Christmas gifts for children in the community. It was a big check."

"I hadn't heard." He shrugged. "But it'll come in handy."

"Yes, it will," Patty answered. "And I see Hailey so it's time for me to go. We're wrapping lights around the frames of the wise men."

"She seems very nice," Breezy said, making conversation as Jake led her into the nursery.

"She's the best. She raised three girls, and did her best to help out at our place."

"Help out?"

He didn't answer. His gaze settled on the door behind her and he frowned. All evidence of the lighthearted Jake Martin disappeared in a matter of seconds.

"Problem?" she asked as she spun around to see what had caught his attention.

"No, not a problem. Just a little brother returned to the fold. I'll have to catch up with you in a few."

He handed Violet over, leaving Breezy the job of wrangling both twins. She held one on each hip and watched him head for the young man who had entered the building, a cowboy hat pushed down on his dark head, his jeans hanging low around slim hips. He had a black eye and a huge scowl on his face. Jake descended on him acting more like an angry parent than an older brother.

That explained more about the man than any questions he might have answered for her. Each time she learned something about this man, it felt as if a tiny chisel had taken aim at her heart, tearing off another small chunk of the armor she'd always thought indestructible.

* * *

Jake didn't know what he planned on saying to Brody. What did you say to a kid that should have been an adult by now? Duke had recently told Jake that the blame for Brody not acting responsible was Jake's fault, because he bailed him out too often. Jake had been too easy on him when it came to the ranch.

It looked like high time someone stopped being easy on Brody. From the looks of things, someone had already taken a piece off his hide. His black eye and the gimpy way he walked said a lot.

"Well?" Jake stopped in front of his younger brother, aware of their audience and not willing to let another Martin family squabble be the thing people remembered about this night. "Head outside."

"I'm not going anywhere with you. I want to see the twins."

"You can see the twins later."

Brody shot a look past him, his smile, complete with dimple, appearing out of nowhere. "Hey, is that the new sister?"

"She isn't our sister."

Brody gave him a knowing look. "I guess that's something to be thankful for."

"I'm not too thankful for anything right now, Brody. What happened to your eye?"

"Aren't you going to ask me about the other guy?" Brody walked away with a casual swagger. Jake followed.

"Who was the other guy?"

"Lincoln," Brody admitted with a shrug. "I'm hungry."

"You're always hungry. Why did you fight with Lincoln?"

"Because he's..." Brody shook his head. "Let it rest. We had a difference of opinion. You might not think much of me. I know I let you down a lot. But I am a Martin and you have taught me that people ought to be treated right. Women ought to be treated right. Lincoln and I had a disagreement and we parted ways permanently."

"That bad?" Jake let go of his frustration with his younger brother.

Brody shrugged, as if it wasn't worth discussing. Jake knew it had to be tough. Lincoln and Brody had been inseparable friends for years. Even when they didn't agree.

"I'm going to get some food," Brody said. "If you don't mind?"

"Go ahead. And mind your manners with Breezy."

Brody stopped and landed a careful look on Jake, even with one eye nearly swollen shut.

"Gotcha, big brother. I'll keep my hands off your…"

"Watch your manners," Jake warned in a growl he hadn't intended.

Man, this is not what he needed, for both his brothers to think that Lawton pushing him and Breezy Hernandez together as the girls' guardians made the two of them a couple. They had been unwillingly forced into a situation neither of them had expected. End of story.

"Of course." Brody tipped his hat and walked away.

Jake shook his head at the retreating back of his younger brother. Nothing really bothered Brody. Or at least it always seemed that way. But whatever had happened with Lincoln had definitely gotten under his skin.

"We're all cleaned up, Uncle Jake," Breezy said as she walked up.

He smiled at Breezy and the twins. He held out his arms and Violet fell into his embrace, her head resting on his shoulder and her thumb instantly going to her mouth. It was getting late, the girls were tired and he still needed to help put up some lights.

"Do you want to take them home with you tonight?" he asked. It made sense. He could get more work done if the girls were in Breezy's care. And neither of them would get work done if they had to wrangle twins all night.

Breezy's eyes widened and she glanced down at the little girl in her arms. "Of course. I think."

"Nervous?"

"No, no, of course not. I can do this."

If he'd guessed her next sentence, the one she hadn't said, it probably would have been something to the effect that she was going to have to do it sooner or later. He agreed. If she was going to be a part of their lives, she would have to get used to having the girls for longer than a few hours at a time.

"You can do it. And if you need anything, I'm just a phone call away." He kissed Violet's cheek. "I'll help you get them in car seats."

"Thank you."

It probably looked easy from the outside, turning those girls over to her. It was anything but.

People probably thought he should be relieved. After all, he'd already helped raise his siblings. He had a ranch and a business to run. Someone taking part of that load should make him happy.

As he walked out the door with Breezy and the twins, he thought of all the reasons why this should be the best thing for him and for the twins, maybe even for her. As he helped carry car seats to her car and helped strap the twins in, he probably should have been thinking that, for this one night, he didn't have to worry.

Instead his worry doubled. Tonight he would worry about all three of them.

# Chapter Seven

On Sunday Breezy pulled into the parking lot of Martin's Crossing Community Church. The main building was a traditional white-sided structure with a tall steeple and stained-glass windows. Next to it was the fellowship and community center, a metal building with a tall wooden cross standing next to it.

After meeting so many of the community members on Friday when she'd helped decorate, it was easier to come here than she had imagined.

Not that she didn't have her doubts. She'd almost talked herself into staying home, but she couldn't. She had promised Jake she would do this. They would go to church as a family. She wanted to make this work for the twins, the two little people counting on her to be in their lives.

This weekend had been a good start. The

twins had stayed with her Friday night and all day Saturday. Yesterday, Jake had stopped by in the late afternoon to pick up the twins but he'd stayed for dinner. After they had finished eating the twins played in the living room. Only one thing had dampened the mood. Once as they all sat in the living room, Violet had looked around and said, "Mama?"

Breezy knew that someday it would hurt less. At that moment, knowing there was no mama and knowing Breezy couldn't fill Elizabeth's shoes, it had hurt.

So for the twins, and maybe for herself, she was going to church. It wasn't that she had something against church, or even against God. She believed. She even prayed. But church, it was all about the past when it came to church.

Someone rapped on her window, and she jumped then frowned at the man smiling at her. He opened the door, cowboy cool in a plaid button-up shirt, jeans and boots. He had shaved off the stubble that had covered his cheeks the previous day. As she stepped out of the car she realized he smelled good, like country air and expensive cologne. A combination she could cuddle up to, if it were any other man. Chivalrous and Old West he might be, but safe? He was anything but safe.

"Nervous?" he asked as she just stood there next to her car.

"A little." She glanced around. "Where are the girls?"

"I've already checked them into the nursery."

"Oh." She studied the building. It felt like looking at her future, all wrapped up in a neat package with a Christmas bow on top. This town, the church, the twins and even Jake.

She wanted to accept it, to believe it. This was her life now. But how many times had she thought she might be able to stay, to put down roots, only to have it ripped out from under her?

Even her life in Oklahoma with her sister.

"You okay?" he asked.

"I'm good."

One brow arched and he studied her face, and then surprised her by reaching for her hand. "Good but a little shaky?"

"You grew up here, didn't you? You've always lived in this town, with these people who know you and this church that has been there for you?"

"Yes, of course."

Of course. Because it was Martin's Crossing. Duke had told her that their great great grandfather had settled this area, building up a farm and starting the general store. And that grandfather's brother had been the law in these parts. Family history.

Breezy's family history was of a drug addict who overdosed and a man whose life story she didn't really know.

"Breezy?"

His voice was soft, husky, and he was standing too close. She pulled herself together and gave him an easy look, the kind she knew how to give. The smile that said she was okay. Everything was good.

"I'm ready," she said. "I have gone to church. I went while I lived in Dawson. It's just…I've had a different experience than you have."

And she was so tired of starting over.

"What was your experience?" he asked as if he really wanted to know. But how did she tell him?

Maria had used churches. She had used Breezy. But how did she explain that to a man who had lived this perfect, American dream kind of life?

He would never understand the embarrassment of being dragged from church to church. He wouldn't get how it felt to sit in a classroom where every other kid had families, homes and nice clothes.

She stopped walking, wondering what to tell him. There was so much about her life that people didn't understand, so she didn't share. Not even with Mia. But she and Jake were raising children together. That changed everything. "My experience was that church was the place where I never really belonged. We were always passing through."

He started to comment but she put a hand up to stop the words that would be some variation of "sorry, shouldn't have been, this will be different." They were facing each other on the sidewalk and somehow her hand settled on his arm.

"This will be different," he assured her. His gaze held hers and he looked like he meant it. And she believed him.

Of course it would be different. She wasn't that dirty little girl anymore. She no longer stood on street corners with her guitar, hoping someone would throw a few dollars in the case. Maria wasn't here, telling her to play along at church, to listen to the stories about God and fishes and loaves, just long enough to get money for a room or food.

The difference between Breezy and Maria was that Maria hadn't believed. She'd only used the people who had been kind enough to put their faith into action. Breezy had wanted to know more. She had wanted to understand the stories, the faith, the hope that the teachers spoke of.

She had always wanted a home, a place to plant roses, maybe a garden. A place to stay. And now she had it, even though it didn't feel like her life. It felt like she was borrowing Lawton's. The idea of staying scared the daylights out of her. And the longer she stayed, the more she grew to love the twins, the more she feared it might all be taken away.

"What should I say?" he asked as they walked toward the building.

"Nothing, really. Just understand that you grew up here, where this was a safe place. I grew up being used by a lady who took me to church to get money."

He nodded, and she was glad that he didn't say anything else. He touched her back and then dropped his hand to his side. The brief gesture cause a shiver to race up her spine.

"I have a roast in the Crock-Pot for lunch," he said as they walked up the steps of the church.

"Is that an invitation?"

"Yes, it's an invitation. It used to be a big family event. There are fewer of us these days but we still have lunch together every Sunday. Today Marty has plans with friends, so it will just be you, me, Duke, Brody and the twins."

"Can I bring something?"

"No, Marty's taken care of everything. And Duke is bringing pie."

Duke's pie. She'd had a slice the other day when she'd had coffee with Jake and it was the best pie she'd ever had. Even better than Vera's at the Mad Cow in Dawson.

They stepped through the doors of the church. A man wearing bib overalls over a dress shirt handed her a bulletin. His gray hair was combed back, and his beard was neatly trimmed. He winked.

"How do you do? I'm Robert Carter."

Breezy took the hand he offered. "I'm Breezy Hernandez."

"Good to know you, miss. And I see you dragged in this scoundrel. How you doing today, Jake? Looks like you're hanging with a better class of people than normal."

"I hope you haven't told Duke he's outclassed," Jake said with a grin.

"I'd say he already knows it." Robert pounded Jake on the shoulder. "You'd best get a seat. And, young lady, watch out for those Martin boys. They're trouble."

Breezy smiled at that as they made their way to the front of the church. Duke was indeed waiting for them. He'd left two seats to his left empty. As they approached he stood, a welcoming look on his face. Breezy breathed a little easier. Duke made people feel at ease. He held a hand out to her and pulled her to the seat next to his.

"Smile, sunshine, or they'll think we're holding you hostage. You know, back in the old days…"

"Don't tell stories, Duke." Jake sat down.

Breezy smiled and took the seat between the two brothers. For a moment there was peace. She glanced around, not wanting to be conspicuous as she surveyed the building. The walls were wood paneled but painted white. A cross hung at the front, behind the pulpit. The band was tuning up. A drummer, guitar player and pianist. Someone stepped forward with a violin.

After a song service that had the church on their feet, the pastor stepped forward. He didn't wear a suit, just jeans and a button-down shirt. His hair was buzzed short and he looked to be not much older than Breezy. But as he spoke, she stopped thinking about his appearance and focused on a message that asked his congregation to really think about what Christmas means to them. Not as Christians, but personally.

How does it change their lives? How does it affect their choices and the way they reach out to others? What makes them different than everyone else in the world?

Breezy leaned in a little, listening to his words. What did Christmas mean to her? As a child it had been a hard time of year, spent in shelters and run-down motels. They'd rarely had a tree. They hadn't spent the day with family, enjoying a big meal. It had been a holiday when churches would reach out to people like Breezy and Maria. She would get a few gifts, maybe new socks and a sweater, sometimes gloves or a jacket. She'd always felt embarrassed taking those gifts, but she'd always wanted them. She'd wanted pretty packages, something new. She'd opened each silly little gift as if it were...

She held her breath and closed her eyes as an image of three wise men kneeling before a baby flashed through her mind.

Duke patted her arm in a brotherly way and told her to take a deep breath. She tried but it came out as a sob. Christmas had changed her life because for one day each year she'd mattered to someone. The kindness of strangers had mattered.

How could she make that difference in other people's lives?

When the service ended, she didn't move, not right away. She needed time to reflect on how, in one message, Christmas had changed for her. Pieces, broken and scattered, had come back together. Jake stood, his blue eyes reflecting understanding.

"Are you okay?"

She nodded. "Yes, I'm good. Thank you."

He nodded and walked away, leaving her alone with her thoughts.

Jake headed for the nursery to get the twins. He should have stayed and said more to Breezy, but he hadn't known what. She'd been sitting there in a prairie skirt, denim jacket and a pastel scarf around her neck, looking like someone who needed a hug. He was the last man for that job.

Duke was there. He was a hugger. They all had their roles in the world. Duke was better at sympathy and compassion. Jake was the brother who made sure everyone was taken care of.

When he walked up to the nursery the girls ran at him, tackling his legs with chubby arms that held tight. The nursery worker, Janet Lester, told him the girls had been good but that Rosie seemed to have the sniffles. He picked both girls up and Rosie did look a little the worse for wear. Her nose was red and her eyes a little misty. Jake's aunt Patty appeared from the back of the nursery, a sympathetic look on her face.

"She's not feeling her normal happy self."

"No, doesn't appear to be," he agreed.

He kissed her forehead the way he'd seen Elizabeth do. Thinking about his sister brought a sharp ache to his heart. His own twin, the person he'd always counted on to share the burden of raising their ragtag family, was gone. Now her little girls needed him to protect them, to raise them and love them.

Without really thinking, he stepped away from the nursery, forgetting for a moment to thank Janet and his aunt Patty. He turned at the last moment and called out to them. They waved and went back to the children whose parents hadn't yet picked them up.

Outside the air was cool but not cold. He headed toward his truck and Duke waylaid him.

"You invited Breezy for lunch, didn't you?"

"I did. Where is she?" He shifted the girls. Duke reached for Violet, taking half the load.

"Talking to Margie Fisher. Margie is in charge of the caroling this year and I mentioned to her that Breezy sings. I thought it might help her to adjust if she felt included. I think they're also discussing the decorating committee. When Margie finds a willing volunteer, she hangs on tight."

"You're not getting her involved. You're throwing her to the wolves."

Duke grinned at that. "Yeah, well, everyone needs to feel included."

"Right." He glanced around and saw Breezy on the sidewalk. Margie stood in front of her, talking nonstop. Margie, with her dark gray dress, neat gray bun and glossy black cane looked like a formidable woman at first glance. But as starched as she appeared on the outside, she was spun sugar on the inside. No one had a bigger heart than Margie Fisher.

Duke tickled Violet and she giggled. Then he blew raspberries on her cheek. She giggled more. Rosie was a dead weight in Jake's arms, sound asleep.

"Rose not feeling good?" Duke asked.

"Doesn't appear to be."

"Take her on home. I can make sure Breezy escapes."

Jake nodded but his gaze caught and held on the woman in question. The wind picked up and she caught her hair and held it back with her hand, but tendrils drifted free and blew across her cheeks. Her hair smelled like sunshine, he knew. It bothered him more than a little that he'd noticed.

But thinking about Breezy was less disturbing than thinking about the sermon that had stabbed at his conscience. Because what was Christmas to him? A time to bring family together? Traditions of a big meal, a tree decorated with ornaments that had been kept for years, maybe generations? What else? Community parties, events that kept them busy for the holiday season?

He let his gaze shift to a man walking out the double doors of the church. Joe with no last name. He'd been in church and now he was walking next to a mom with two small children. Jake didn't know their names.

"I have to go. Can you hand Violet over to Breezy? I think she has a car seat in her car."

"Sure thing. I have car seats, too. We're all prepared. Is Brody at the house?"

"Yeah, at least he was when I left. See you there."

"Yep." Duke shifted Violet to his other arm and the two waved goodbye as Jake headed out with Rosie.

The young mom and Joe were still walking, the kids staying close to their mom as she tried to shelter them from the rain. Joe took off his jacket to hold it over the little ones. Jake hurried to his truck, unlocked the door and buckled Rose in the car seat.

A few minutes later, he pulled up next to Joe, the mom and those two kids. The rain was falling a little harder now. He rolled down the window and they all looked at him. Joe smiled and tipped that bent-up hat he wore. The mom, who might have been in her early twenties, looked worn down.

"Do you need a ride?" he offered, leaning a little to look down at the two kids, who had backed away but were grinning like the idea of riding in his truck was the coolest thing ever.

The mom started to shake her head but Joe opened the back door of the truck and the kids piled in, wet hair and damp clothes. "Of course she does. It's really coming down and she lives a half mile out. I told her someone would give her a ride."

"Of course," Jake agreed. "Joe, you get in, too."

"I don't have far to go," Joe answered. The mom had climbed in the front. Jake pushed the armrest back to open the middle seat. She scooted and Joe stood, unsure.

"Nevertheless…" Jake paused. "We have roast on at the house. There's plenty for all of us."

"I'd never turn down roast." Joe pulled himself into the truck. "Thank you, Jake."

Jake glanced back over his shoulder where the boys had buckled in, looking drenched and cold. He introduced himself to the young woman, who was trying hard to tell him he didn't need to feed them. He cranked up the heat.

"No reason to let a good roast go to waste," he argued back. "Unless you have other plans."

She shook her head and her arms went around her two boys. "No, sir, we don't have other plans."

What did his faith mean to him? He glanced

at the man sitting next to him and the three people in the backseat and he wondered if he'd have thought to give them a ride last week. How had he gotten so wrapped up in his own life that he'd stopped thinking to look around him?

And what had made a difference this week? A sermon? Or the woman sitting next to him during that sermon? A woman he didn't know that well, but knew without a doubt would have driven this unlikely four to their destination and fed them along the way.

# Chapter Eight

Breezy followed Duke, who'd offered to carry Violet, through the house. She'd been in Jake's house before but only as far as the office. Today she walked down a wide stone-tiled hallway to the kitchen. The home was stone and log on the outside, and the interior walls were the same. The massive kitchen looked like a restaurant. The counter formed an L-shaped bar around the cooking area. Bar stools were arranged around the counter. There was a wood-plank-style dining room table in the open section with French doors that led to a deck overlooking the hills in the distance.

The room was already crowded with people. She smiled at Brody, whom she hadn't been officially introduced to. He had Rose in his arms and was tickling her until she bent over, giggling. Joe was stirring something on the stove.

A young mom and two little boys were sitting at the counter bar looking half-scared and out of place. Breezy gave her best encouraging smile and the mom shrugged thin shoulders.

"Hey, looks like a houseful!" Duke grinned big and the little boys shrank against their mom. Of course they did. It wasn't every day a kid learned about Goliath at church and then went to lunch with someone that looked like he might *be* Goliath.

Breezy stepped next to the giant. "Ease up, you're a little bit scary."

He glanced down at her. "I'm handsome, not scary."

He grinned again at those little boys.

"No," she countered, "you're scary. If I didn't know you, I'd want a slingshot and some rocks."

He laughed at that. "Breezy, I've been described a lot of ways, but you're the first to call me a Philistine."

"Well, if the shoe fits." She glanced at his feet. "But do they make shoes that fit?"

He laughed again, then the two little boys laughed and their mom broke into a hesitant smile. Breezy stepped away from the friendly giant. "I'm Breezy, and you are?"

"Cora," the mom spoke softly. "And these are my boys, Ben and Jason."

"It's really nice to meet you guys."

"Do you live here?" the smaller of the two asked.

"No, I don't. I'm just…" What was she, exactly? She sensed the boy wasn't the only one waiting for her answer. She glanced at Jake. He stood at the counter but he'd turned to watch her, those blue eyes narrowed, waiting to see what she'd say.

Was she just visiting? Passing through? She met his eyes and he arched a brow, pushing her to answer.

"I live down the road." She finally settled on the easier explanation.

She let her gaze settle on Jake, and saw from the corner of her eye that Duke was giving him a look. She had an ally in Duke, she knew that. He'd told her that the twins needed her. She sometimes thought they might.

"If someone would set the table, this is almost ready." Jake shifted the direction of her thoughts with the proclamation.

"I can do that," Breezy offered. She turned slowly, looking at the abundance of cabinets. "If you'll tell me where to find plates."

He pointed and she opened the cabinet. Cora slid off the stool, telling her boys to stay put. "Can I get the glasses ready or anything?"

Jake pointed to another cabinet. "Glasses up there, ice in the fridge door and tea is already made."

It felt like a family gathering, Breezy thought. Brody was entertaining the twins. Duke was cutting pie and Joe was moving serving dishes to the table. She thought she could learn to feel like a part of this life, this family. Even though they weren't quite a family. Cora and her boys, Joe and even Breezy were strays brought in out of the rain.

As they settled down to eat, Jake's phone rang. He apologized and answered it. As he spoke, he glanced at Breezy. He nodded, said it would be okay and then ended the call.

"Who was that?" Brody asked as he piled roast on bread.

"Marty." Jake passed salad to Cora.

"And?" Brody pushed.

Breezy wondered how he could have been raised in this home and not realize it was a bad idea to push Jake. She considered kicking his shin since she sat closest.

Jake sighed, shook his head and passed the plate of bread. "She is stuck in San Antonio for a few days. Her sister is in the hospital."

"Oh, that's rough. You, the ranch, twins." Brody whistled as he poured gravy over the food on his plate.

Breezy watched the mound of food grow and looked from the plate to the man sitting next to her. Not that Brody was a man. He had to be close to her age but he seemed younger. He wasn't tall like Jake and Duke, and he was lean and wiry. But he obviously could pack away the food.

He caught her staring at his plate and grinned. "You don't think I can eat it?"

"I have a feeling you will," she countered.

He laughed and dug in. Jake cleared his throat. "I don't think we've prayed."

Everyone stopped. Jake reached for the hands of the people on either side of him and around the table hands joined. They all bowed their heads. As Jake prayed a blessing on the food, Breezy prayed she'd survive.

After the meal was finished and the dishes were done, Duke offered to give Cora, Joe and the boys a ride back to town. Brody disappeared with the excuse that he had work to do in the barn. Breezy watched as little by little everyone left. The twins were sleeping. It was just her and Jake. And he looked restless.

"Is there a problem?"

"A small one," he admitted.

"Okay, well, why don't you tell me? Or is this another rule, 'don't question Jake'? Or is there a rule that you have to do everything on your own without help?"

She was goading him, she knew. But she didn't know any other way to get the man to open up, to let her in. Not that she really needed or wanted all of his deep, dark secrets. As a matter of fact, after thinking about it, she was considering pushing Rewind and leaving him to his misery.

As she considered making her exit, he sighed and brushed a hand through his hair, leaving the dark brown strands in disarray. When he looked at her, his blue eyes were troubled. Okay, she did care. He needed someone to take part of the load or he'd work himself into an early grave.

The person to do that was her.

"Tell me," she spoke softly. "Listen, I know you love your family, but you can't do it all alone. What good will you be to the twins if you don't take care of yourself?"

"You're probably right."

"I know I'm right." She said and for some crazy reason took a step closer. Why? Why did she suddenly feel the need to comfort this man? Jake Martin wasn't a man who invited hugs and easy touches. But she touched him anyway.

She put her palm on the smooth planes of his face, aware that she should step back, aware that the room had gone still except the wild pounding of her heart. He didn't move away; in fact his hand slid to her waist and pulled her close. For a long moment they stood toe to toe, forehead to forehead, her hand on his cheek, his hand on her hip.

Breezy knew that they were both waiting for common sense to return. But it didn't. Slowly, ever so slowly, his head bent toward hers and their lips touched. He kissed her slowly, taking his time it seemed, and she closed her eyes.

She moved her hands to the back of his neck. He raised his head for a brief moment then leaned in again, brushing his lips against hers and then moving to her cheek.

The front door slammed. Jake stepped back, releasing her from his hold. She stared up at him, waiting for him to say something, to undo the moment. He didn't. He gave her a long look, rubbing his hand against the back of his neck, and then he put distance between them.

Breezy thought she might cry.

Jake had stepped away from Breezy but it hadn't been an easy thing to do. It should have been. He should have stepped back, said a polite "thank you for the kiss" and let it end. Instead he stood there looking at her, wondering if there would be a repeat, and kind of wishing for one.

That proved he hadn't been getting enough

sleep. He rubbed his hand across the back of his neck, ignoring his brother. Brody shot the two of them a curious look and mumbled something about his horse and antibiotics. Jake guessed he should listen but didn't.

"Jake, the problem?" Breezy called him back to planet Earth with that question. She was right, they'd been discussing a problem.

"Right. Marty won't be home for a few days. And I'd been counting on her to help with the twins."

Breezy's eyes narrowed and her pretty mouth, the one he'd just kissed, formed a straight line of disapproval. "You understand that you're not raising the twins alone anymore? There is a will, I think, and it appointed us both guardians."

Brody hurried past them, head down, hands up. "I'm a neutral party but she's right."

"Get out of here," Jake growled.

Brody obliged.

Breezy didn't give him a chance to interrupt. "You're arrogant, Jake Martin. You have this idea that you are the only person capable of doing anything. You run this ranch. You run your family. You are now trying to run me, and that isn't going to work because I'm not yours to run."

"I kind of got that."

"No, I don't think you have gotten it. You're worried about how you'll take care of this ranch, take care of the twins, and probably worried about taking care of me. Well, I can take care of myself. And I think I can even help you take care of those two little girls." She hesitated, locking those caramel-brown eyes on him. "*Our* little girls, Jake. As much as it hurts, they are ours."

It did hurt. Hurt enough that it felt as if she'd physically pushed him. He took a deep breath that shuddered on the exhale. She started toward him but he held his hands up to stop her.

"I'm sorry." She said it softly and it felt like rain coming down on him. "I'm sorry that you lost your sister and I'm sorry you lost Lawton. We're in this together, though. And you have to let me help you. Maybe that's what Lawton wanted. Maybe he knew you'd need someone from outside the family who couldn't be bullied and who maybe, just maybe, would bully you back."

Had Lawton thought that? It made sense, but Jake couldn't delve into the psychology of Lawton's plan. Not now.

"I have to take cattle to an auction tomorrow and I need to make sure the guys move a herd from one field to another. I also have to make contact with a firm in Fort Worth. Lawton and

I were putting a system in their office and it has a few kinks. I was counting on Marty."

"Yeah, I get that. Now you'll count on me."

"Right, I'll count on you."

She smiled at that. "See, that wasn't so hard. Now, why don't we get their bags packed and you can bring them over this afternoon?"

He agreed to her plan. What other choice did he have?

Later, as he pulled up to Lawton's house, he realized it was the only option. And it was the right choice to make. She shared custody with him and it was time for him to let go. As he looked at the house, he realized it was time to stop calling it Lawton's house. It was Breezy's house now. It was her car in the drive. It was Breezy who would open the door when he walked up the steps with the girls.

She was right, it was time to face that Lawton and Elizabeth weren't coming home. This wasn't temporary. The girls were his. They were Breezy's.

Accepting reality meant accepting her in his life. It also meant he'd have to trust that she wasn't going to sneak away in the night. That thought unsettled him a little. He could see that the twins needed her. They were getting used to her songs, to her hugs, to the way she talked to them.

As he'd known she would, she greeted him on the front porch, taking Rose from him. She kissed the little girl's cheek and then leaned to kiss Violet's cheek.

"All ready for this?" he asked as they walked through the front door.

"I think so. I have real food and I put clean sheets on their beds. I'm a little worried how they'll adjust to sleeping in their beds again."

"They usually do better if they sleep in one crib together," he offered.

"Oh, I should have thought of that."

"It isn't something that makes or breaks you, Breezy. But it might make your night a little better."

They walked into the living room. Violet and Rosie were fresh from their nap and ready to play. Violet wiggled from his arms and Rosie was already pulling a doll from the basket of toys next to the couch. He looked around the room, noticing that it still looked exactly as it had when she'd moved in.

"You know, you can change things. Put out your own stuff." Weren't women big on personal touches?

She glanced around the room and then looked back at him and shrugged. "I know. It's a strange concept for me. I've never really had a place of my own and I guess I still think of this as Lawton's house that I'm staying in. Like he and Elizabeth will be back. They'll want their lives, their girls…"

She covered her face with her hands and shook her head.

Jake pulled her close. Her hands were still on her face and her arms were between them. She sobbed as he held her. He guessed they both had some adjusting to do. He stroked long blond hair until she stopped crying.

"Shh, it'll get easier. We both have to figure this out."

She nodded into his shoulder, her head resting there, fitting perfectly. Common sense, which had been in short supply lately, told him to pull back. But she felt good in his arms and he didn't want to let go, not yet.

The twins were playing, sitting close together the way they sometimes did, heads practically touching, their dolls between them. He wondered if they communicated that way. Did they discuss the situation, wonder together where their mommy and daddy had gone to? Those thoughts ached inside him and suddenly he needed this woman in his arms as much as she needed him.

Eventually he let her go and she wiped her eyes and sniffled. "I'm sorry."

"No need to apologize." He sank onto the sofa and watched as she took a seat in the rocking chair. "Breezy, we have to accept this. I have to work on letting you be my partner in raising the girls. You have to make this your home."

She seemed pale in the dim light of the lamp and her eyes shimmered. She eventually nodded. "I know."

"A home where you stay," he pushed.

Because that was still his fear, that the twins would get attached and she'd leave.

"Why do you think I'll leave?"

"I know you aren't used to staying in one place."

She shook her head, leaning a little in his direction. "Yes, that's been true for most of my life. But for most of my life I didn't have a reason to stay. But your trust issues, those are your issues to work through."

"Trust issues?" So in a matter of days she thought she knew him?

"I've been here almost a week and…it's a small town." She caught her bottom lip between her teeth and studied him for a minute.

"Yes, it's a small town." Suddenly he was uncomfortable with the direction this conversation had taken.

"I know about your mom, and I know that when she left, you took care of things. You were just a boy and…"

He held up a hand. "Don't start picturing me as a little boy in need of a mother. I was twelve and I survived."

"Of course you did," she said. "You and I have that in common. And now we have those two little girls counting on us to help them survive."

He stood, because it was time for him to go. He wanted to be upset, because leave it to a woman to think a man had to get in touch with his emotions in order to deal with life. He wasn't upset, though. Because Breezy pushed him in a way that few people did. The twins needed her strength. Maybe he did, too.

"Jake, I'm sorry." Her hand reached for his. He looked down at those fingers with pale pink polish holding on to his, not letting go.

"Don't be," he finally answered. "We'll get through this. But I'm just about talked out so I'm going to head to the house and get some work done."

"I'll see you tomorrow." She stood on tiptoe and kissed his cheek before he went out the door.

Jake got in his truck and headed back to the ranch, to work left undone. His phone rang as he drove. A county deputy was on the other end, letting him know they'd checked out a few leads on the break-in but so far weren't any closer to figuring out who might have been at Lawton's the other day. They had one print, a half print actually, and it wasn't in the system.

Great. One more thing to worry about.

# Chapter Nine

Breezy and the twins were gone. Jake walked through Lawton's place two days later, looking, listening. He could admit to a good case of the nerves settling over him the minute he'd walked through the door, calling out to Breezy and the twins and getting no reply. Her car was in the drive. He'd checked the garage and the truck was parked where it had been for weeks.

He walked out the back door and headed in the direction of the barn. Halfway there he heard laughter, Breezy's and the twins'. The sound drifted on the wind and seemed to come from the field behind the house. He opened the gate and paused, waiting for more laughter, maybe conversation that might lead him in the right direction. After several seconds he heard Breezy yell, "Timber!"

That did it. He ran in the direction of her

voice, coming to a sudden stop as he spotted her, the twins and an Arizona cypress toppling to the ground. She stood a good distance back from the tree. The twins were in a wagon that had been kept in the garage. She was holding the handle of the wagon with one hand and a saw in the other. When she spotted him she waved the saw and then pointed to the fallen tree.

"What are you doing?" He smiled at Rosie and Violet. "You girls having fun?"

Rosie nodded. Violet pointed to the tree, her mouth open and her eyes wide. "Tree," they both said.

"Yes, a Christmas tree." Breezy looked far too pleased and that only annoyed him more.

"What in the world are you thinking?"

"That if I'm going to make this house my home, I need a tree." She looked surprised and a little bit annoyed.

"I could have gotten you a tree. As a matter of fact, there's probably one in the attic."

"I wanted a real tree. I've never had one."

She brushed at a few strands of hair blowing in the wind even though she wore a cap pulled down tight. Her eyes were bright toffee and her pink lips parted in an excited grin.

How did she do that? How did she look like a child and a fantastically gorgeous woman all at the same time? He allowed himself a minute to look at her, at all of that blond hair flowing out from beneath a white knit cap. She'd worn an old canvas coat, probably Lawton's, with a white sweater, jeans and brown riding boots.

"Anyway," she was saying, "I thought it wouldn't be hard to cut one down. I hope it's okay to do that."

"Yes, it's okay." It wasn't okay to turn him inside out this way. It wasn't okay to look like a woman he wanted to kiss. Again.

None of this was okay and Lawton should have known better. He was angry. Angry with himself, with her for being so tempting, and angry with Lawton for leaving them alone in this mess.

"Jake?"

He brushed a hand over his face and then raised that same hand to stop her. He just needed a minute. She started to say something. He held up one finger. Surely she could understand. He needed a minute. One quiet minute to get past the loss of a sister and his best friend.

He needed more quiet moments to figure out what exactly she was doing to his calm, very ordered existence.

When he opened his eyes, she was still watching him and the twins were staring, as well. They wore identical looks of doubt. Of course they did. All three of them were doubting his sanity and his ability to take care of them. And that's what got him. Lawton hadn't added a partner, he'd added one more person Jake felt the need to care for.

The empty house had shaken him. He tried to write off this roller coaster of emotions as fear. He hadn't expected to find her gone. He had panicked. But they were fine.

"Let's get that tree back to the house." He pulled gloves out of his jacket pocket and put them on. Without anything further said, he grabbed the end of the tree and trudged along next to Breezy, who pulled the wagon.

"I'm sorry," she whispered halfway to the house. The twins had climbed out of the wagon and were walking alongside the tree, telling him in their toddler voices that they could help.

"No need to be sorry." He said it with an ease that surprised him. "You wanted a tree. I should have gotten you a tree."

She glanced at him then. She looked mad. Maybe close to furious. They didn't know each other, didn't know the right words to say or what the other person was thinking.

When people had children together, it was a given that they would know each other. He and Breezy were walking through a field of land mines.

"I don't need for you to get me a tree, Jake. I don't need you to take care of me. That isn't why I'm here. Lawton didn't leave me to you. He didn't ask you to take care of me, too. I'm here to help you. I've taken care of myself for a long, long time."

"Right, of course."

"Jake, I'm not the kind of woman that needs a man to run to my rescue. I won't ask you to hang curtains, kill wasps or slay dragons."

He wondered why she was so against allowing a man to do those things for her. He didn't ask. Asking would have dragged him further into her life. She was kind enough to give him an out and he should take it.

He dropped the tree in the yard. He would have to find a stand for it. And she'd have to clear a space in the living room. He would have explained but she trudged up the steps ahead of him. The twins following close behind.

As they entered the house he noticed what he hadn't before. It smelled wonderful. The kinds of smells that made his stomach rumble with hunger.

She must have heard because she laughed. "You're welcomed to stay for dinner."

"That isn't tofu, is it?"

She shook her head as he followed her to the kitchen. "No, it's bread and homemade stew."

"You cook?"

She nodded and lifted the lid from the slow cooker. "I'm learning. I've never had a kitchen of my own, not really. In Dawson I worked a lot, waitressing, and I ate at the restaurant. Before that I lived in California in an efficiency that was less than efficient. It was one room with a bed, microwave and dorm-size fridge."

"Why did you stay there?"

She stirred the stew and then took a careful taste. He waited for an answer and wondered if it was too much to ask. Maybe they didn't need to know each other's stories. But then, she knew his.

"I stayed because I didn't know what else to do. I don't have a real education so I couldn't get a decent job. My income kept me where I was."

"You didn't call your sister?"

She shook her head. "I was five when Maria took me. I didn't remember Mia's last name. I didn't know where she'd been taken to."

"What happened to Maria?"

The lid clanged a little on the cooker. She righted it and set the spoon on a plate. "She died when I was nineteen." She cleared her throat. "This will be ready in an hour. Let's put the tree up."

"Breezy..."

She shook her head. "No. Let's stop with the

past. We all have one and we all have to make choices about how we live today, how we live tomorrow. I've had great experiences and bad experiences. I define who I am today."

"Experiences do change who we are."

"Right, but they don't have to destroy us. Those experiences don't have to take our joy or make us afraid to take chances."

"I guess you're right."

She grinned and he noticed the slight dimple in her left cheek. "I know I'm right."

After Jake put the tree in a stand, he disappeared into the garage to find ornaments. Breezy brought a box from the kitchen and set it on the table. The twins peered inside, smiling and reaching for the decorations they'd made with dough. She'd found the recipe in an old cookbook, one that said it had belonged to Lawton's grandmother. At last she'd found family recipes. It made her feel connected. She'd had a grandmother. She had a past, ancestors, connections. She now had what so many people took for granted: her history.

"What's this?" Jake returned carrying a tub that he sat on the floor next to the tree. He sat down on the sofa and watched as she strung ribbon through holes in the baked and decorated dough decorations.

"We made these." She handed a star to Rosie and a tree to Violet.

Jake picked one up, tapped it, held it to his mouth. Breezy watched, not sure he would actually take a bite. Surely he wouldn't. He started to.

"Don't eat it!"

He pulled it back and shot a look at the twins. Both girls wore big grins and now had their decorations up to their mouths, ornery looks in their blue eyes.

"No eating, girls," he said in mock seriousness.

They giggled at him, all three of them. Breezy wanted the moment to go on. She wanted to decorate a tree, maybe drink hot cocoa and eat the cookies she'd also made that morning. Maybe this would become a tradition, their tradition.

"So we have a tub full of decorations and yet you felt inclined to make your own?" he asked as he pulled lights and a few other decorations from the tub.

She shrugged slim shoulders and he noticed a faint pink in her cheeks. "It seemed like the thing to do."

"Making decorations?" He really didn't get it. Maybe he didn't need to.

"I found the recipe in a family cookbook and there were paints and glitter in a craft room upstairs. I hope that's okay." She had felt strange, wandering through the house last night after the girls had gone to sleep.

"Of course it is. I'll repeat, you live here."

Yes, it was her house, but it wasn't. The craft room had an abundance of supplies and a half-finished toddler-size dress on the sewing machine. The bedroom that had belonged to Lawton and Elizabeth still had towels hanging next to the shower.

She'd found family photo albums with pictures of her father, his parents, his siblings. There were pictures of Lawton with his parents. She'd sat for a long time with that photo album, picturing herself in their lives and being unable to, because she hadn't existed to them.

But she had her own life. She had memories of who she had been and where she had lived. It was tough but she had to blend who she had always been with the person she now knew herself to be. The daughter of a senator.

"Let's decorate the tree." She stood, ready to let go of the thoughts that brought her nothing but regret. She reached for the ornament she'd bought at Oregon's shop.

"That's new." Jake took a closer look.

She nodded and hung the ornament up high on a sturdy branch. "Do you want to string lights before we get too far into the process of hanging decorations?"

"Sounds like a plan." He opened the tub and pulled out a box of lights. "You'll have to help."

She shifted away from the tree and noticed the girls were still sitting with their decorations. They looked perfectly innocent.

"You girls sit and as soon as the lights are up, we'll hang your ornaments."

They smiled at her, perfectly sweet smiles. She looked to Jake. He glanced at the girls, then at her. "Suspicious."

"Very." She shrugged it off. "If you go behind the tree you can string them on that side and pass the lights for me to wrap around this side."

From her side of the tree she watched as he started the lights at the top of the tree and then wrapped them around, handing them off to her. She took the lights and wrapped them around the front, passing back to him. And down the tree they worked. At times their hands would touch briefly and she would wonder how this would be in a year or five years. What if he found someone and married?

What would it be like if he had his own family? Would he still include her and the twins? Would they all get together on holidays? Would the twins spend half of their time with him and his family? Round and round the thoughts went, like the lights being wrapped around the tree, and she had to stop.

"Where'd you go, Hernandez?" He pushed the string of lights at her.

"I'm here."

"You're quiet." He handed her the strand of lights for the last time.

She finished and the two of them stepped back to survey their work after Jake plugged the lights in. The clear lights twinkled and the tree was beautiful, even with just the one ornament in place. The twins were in awe. At least for a moment.

"Come on, girls, let's hang your ornaments." Breezy held out the box to Jake and he took several. "You get the top half."

Violet and Rosie hung their ornaments side by side and came back for more. Violet took an angel. Rosie took a shepherd. Each time they hung their ornaments side by side, jabbering in a language only they understood.

Jake pulled another box of ornaments from the tub. He handed Breezy one that told the birthday of the twins and their names on one side. On the other it had a picture of them as newborns. She hung it closer to the top so it wouldn't fall and get broken. Jake hung a snowflake with a family picture—Lawton, Elizabeth and the twins.

Each ornament felt like a piece of history, a piece of her family. As Jake finished, holding the twins to hang decorations on the higher branches, Breezy stepped back to survey the job they'd done. Jake caught her eye and she gave him a thumbs-up before picking up the box with the nativity Lefty Mueller had given her. She touched the hand-carved pieces, took them out and arranged them on the fireplace mantel with Christmas lights behind them. Jake came to stand near her right shoulder.

"One of Lefty's?"

She nodded as she watched the lights twinkle and the nativity caught the soft glow. "Yes."

"It's beautiful."

"Yes, it is. I've always wanted one." It was one of her contributions to their new traditions, but he wouldn't understand. He wouldn't understand what it meant to have keepsake ornaments, a nativity and something handmade with the twins to keep year after year.

This was the place where she would stay. She would be here next year to carry on these traditions with Rosie and Violet.

She would create memories for all of them. And stability that made them feel safe each night, not afraid to sleep, not afraid of where they would be the next day or next week. She would give them everything she'd never had, including family.

"I think we should finish the tree and then eat, because I'm starving," Jake suggested. They stood shoulder to shoulder. He touched his fingers to hers.

Something came over her. She wanted to lean against him, put her head on his shoulder. Instead she pulled away, coming to her senses. Better late than never.

"Yes, we should definitely eat."

"I think the twins are having an appetizer." He nodded toward the girls. "They're eating your popcorn."

She laughed at the sight that greeted her as she turned. The twins were sitting on the floor with popcorn she'd spent the previous evening stringing to make a garland for the tree. As they kept a careful eye on the adults, they nibbled kernels of popped corn off the string.

"I hope you weren't planning to use that again next year," Jake teased.

"No, I hadn't planned on it. And I think our helpers are definitely ready to eat."

Traditions started this way, she thought. As she sat at the table she also realized that Christmas was far more than these traditions. But the traditions reminded people of the real meaning of the holiday.

Throughout the Bible people had held to traditions and celebrations in order to remember what God had done for them. Passover, Hanukkah, Palm Sunday, Easter each holiday held a tradition that was a reminder of God at work.

For Christmas, the tree, the lights, the nativity, all were reminders, but the real meaning went so much deeper. And this year the reminder touched a little deeper because Breezy could look at the people sitting with her at that table and she could see what God had done for her.

He'd given her what she'd always wanted. She had a family. She had a home. She even had a plant. The poinsettia Joe had given sat in the center of the table, a reminder that she was staying. People who stayed had plants.

After they finished dinner, Jake helped by clearing the table and doing dishes. Breezy gave the girls their bath. He found them when they were out of the tub and wearing matching pink gowns and matching polka-dot robes. He peeked in the room they shared and waved.

Breezy ran a comb through Violet's hair. "They're ready for a story and then bed."

"I could make coffee while you get them down."

"I'd prefer hot tea," she answered.

The conversation was so normal it took her

by surprise. They weren't a couple. They didn't end their evenings with coffee and discussion of the day's events. As kind as Jake might be, she knew he still didn't trust her. She knew he had his own life and she was added baggage.

"I can make hot tea," he offered.

"You don't have to. I mean, if you have things you need to do." But she was lonely and company, any company, would be so nice. The closer they got to Christmas, the more she missed Mia and the people she'd met in Oklahoma.

"I don't have anywhere I have to be." He leaned against the door frame. "Do you have a hot date?"

She snorted at that. He really didn't know her. "I don't date."

"Interesting." One dark brow arched and she turned her attention back to the girls. "Is that a warning?"

He should go now. She thought about telling him to leave. But the twins were pulling away from her, wanting their uncle Jake.

"No, not a warning at all. It's a simple statement."

He grinned and she was startled by how much that smile of his changed everything.

"I think Lawton might have thought…"

She pulled Rosie back to her lap. "Lawton couldn't have planned that."

He shrugged, picked up Violet and hugged her before setting her back on the ground. Both of them were silent. They looked at each other and looked at the twins.

"Herbal tea," she reminded. He exited the room and she was left with the girls, with tears she tried to hide and with doubts. So many doubts.

Each day got a little easier as she got to know the twins and understand this new life. But each day also grew a little more complicated as she got to know Jake and felt her heart moving a little in his direction.

Jake was the kind of man most women dreamed about. She'd had her share of dreams over the years. Long, long ago she'd thought maybe someday a man would rescue her. But dreams were not reality. Men like Jake didn't date women like Breezy. They didn't take the girl home to meet the family, or even want the family to know about her.

As she joined him in the kitchen, she reminded herself it was nothing more than a cup of tea and a minute to catch up. They would do a lot of this in the coming years. Now was the time to adjust and accept his presence in her life.

# *Chapter Ten*

On Thursday evening Breezy made it to town for the choir practice Margie Fisher had asked her to be a part of. She had wrangled the twins into warm clothes, fed them pasta and green beans. She'd even managed to do the dishes and throw in a load of laundry.

And she was exhausted. She had always thought children would be a lot of work. She knew babies took time and love. She didn't know that *two* could turn a person's world upside down and inside out. As she'd tried to put one girl in pants, the other had taken off running, giggling and losing hair clips as she made her escape. She'd chased Violet with Rosie under her arms and managed to snag her only to have Rosie escape and run through the house like a wild thing on the loose.

At Oregon's All Things shop she parked,

got out of the car and for a minute she stood there, unwilling to unbuckle the twins from their car seats. She closed her eyes and took a deep breath, needing a moment to give her strength to get through this night. She had no idea how Marty managed, but she now realized the woman deserved a medal.

She wasn't a quitter, but the girls had definitely worn her out. A part of her had almost expected them to tie her up and ransack the house! A quick peek in the window of the car led her to wonder how such innocent little girls could wreak such havoc on a house!

She leaned back against the car. A few deep breaths and she'd be ready for round two.

"Hey, you okay?"

She opened her eyes and saw Oregon. "I'm good. Just needed a breather."

"Those twins are something else, aren't they?"

She nodded and closed her eyes again. The air was cool and the sun had set, leaving a dusky, lavender light on the western horizon. She worried that if Oregon said anything too sympathetic, she might actually cry. It had been that kind of day. The kind that made her wonder if she was really cut out for raising two little girls.

The western horizon reminded her of times in the past when Maria would say, *I think it's time for a new adventure.*

Sometimes Breezy had looked forward to those adventures. And other times she'd wanted to just stay, to let her feet stay rooted in that spot, let it become familiar.

"Breezy?"

"I'm good. I'll get them out and meet you at the church?"

Oregon closed the shop door. Breezy noticed then that her daughter, Lilly, was with her. Lilly grinned and held up a puppy.

"Want one?" Lilly asked. "They're nearly weaned and Mom said I can't keep any of them. Well, except the mama dog, Belle."

"What kind are they?" She opened the car door and started to unbuckle Rosie. Oregon moved to the other side of the car and did the same with Violet.

"They're mutts," Oregon offered. "The mother is a border collie. Dad is anyone's guess."

Breezy glanced back at the fawn-and-white puppy that Lilly was holding. The girl had moved closer and her blue eyes fairly twinkled. Breezy studied the girl more closely, taking in her dark hair, her blue eyes. Interesting. She smiled and refocused on the puppy.

"How long did you say you've lived here?" she asked Oregon.

"Breezy, the puppies are almost weaned. I'm sure the twins would love one." Oregon returned to the subject of puppies. "Really, a person with twins should have a puppy. That border collie half might be good at keeping these little girls rounded up." Oregon bit down on her bottom lip and gave Breezy a look. The subject of puppies was safe. The subject of Lilly was off-limits.

"A puppy, huh?" She looked back at the dog again, noticing its slightly long hair, gentle brown eyes and the way it leaned into Lilly. "I've never had a pet."

Lilly practically gasped. "No way."

"Yes way," Breezy confirmed. "I've never had a dog or a cat. I've never stayed anywhere long enough to have an animal."

"You're not going anywhere this time, Breezy." Oregon had Violet out of the seat and was kissing her cheek. "I love these little girls."

"Me, too," Breezy said. They were a part of her. They weren't little strangers shoved into her life. They were her flesh and blood, her DNA. They were her family.

Oregon joined her and the five of them, plus the puppy, headed down the sidewalk in the direction of the church. Lilly put the puppy down and held its pink leash as they crossed the road. The little dog wagged her fluffy tail and sniffed the ground as they walked.

"You don't have to take a puppy," Oregon offered.

"I think I'd like to have one. Is it a boy or a girl?"

"That one is a girl. We call her Daisy, but you can call her whatever you like."

"Daisy." Breezy looked at the dog and the girl holding the leash. "I'll take her when she's weaned."

As they walked, Joe joined them on the sidewalk. He was wearing his usual tan jacket, tan pants and work boots, his bent-up hat pulled down on his thin gray hair. But today he looked tired. His skin looked as gray as his hair.

"Are you okay, Joe?" Breezy asked as he stepped next to her.

He peered at Oregon, who didn't really seem to notice. "I'm good, thank you. And you, Breezy? How is motherhood?"

"Exhausting."

"I'm sure it is. Although I've never been a mother." He smiled at that. "And I wasn't able to be a father to the one child I had."

"I'm sorry, Joe." Breezy shifted Rosie, who was squirming in her arms to get down.

"No one's fault but my own. I let too many years go by. Years I'm sorry for. I hope to someday make it up to her."

Breezy studied the older man in the dim light of the street lamp. "I think we all live with some regrets."

"Yes, I suppose we do. But this is Christmas. It's a time of hope. It's a time of celebrating our faith. Because without this one event, what would we have hope in? We have a lot to be thankful for. And you, Miss Oregon." Joe shifted to look at the other woman, his eyes gentle. "How are things at your shop?"

Oregon's smile came with hesitancy. "It's better. The Christmas traffic has helped."

"Keep your chin up, my dear. Don't give up hope."

"Yes," she responded, but Breezy didn't think that Oregon looked all that hopeful.

The light display in the park next to the church lit up the entire block, lending a glow of twinkling lights to the darkening sky. The nativity graced the center of the display and music played from a speaker inside the manger.

"Where will you spend Christmas, Joe?" Breezy asked as they walked up to the church. Lilly had run off to talk to friends, dragging the dog that was soon to be Breezy's with her.

"I'm sure I'll find somewhere to spend the holidays. Of course I'll be here for the town celebration the night before Christmas Eve. And then maybe I'll go somewhere warm."

"You should be with friends or family." She put Rosie down and held the child's hand. "I'm sure you could spend the day with us."

He touched her arm. "I appreciate that, Breezy. It's good to know I have friends. And you, Oregon, what will you do for the holidays?"

Oregon held Violet's hand now and she looked up, surprised and unsure. "Lilly and I will be together."

Breezy reached for her hand. "Spend the day with us."

"You don't have to do that." Oregon held tight to Violet, who was pulling to get away.

"But I have a home." Breezy reached for Violet and held both twins so they couldn't escape. "I've never had a home to invite friends to."

"But what about the Martins?" Oregon reminded.

"What about the Martins?" Jake walked up behind her. She spun to face him, the twins giggling at the movement.

"Oh, I… We were discussing Christmas."

"And?" Jake reached for Rosie and Breezy allowed him to take the child.

"Oregon and Joe don't have family in the area."

Jake looked from Joe to Oregon. "I see. Of course they're welcome to join us at the ranch for Christmas."

"I wouldn't want to impose," Oregon assured him with Joe echoing the sentiment.

"No imposition. We'll all be together. There's always room for a few more."

A few more. Including her.

She felt unsettled at the thought. The twins were her family. She didn't know how to fit into Jake's family. He had an aunt and uncle, cousins, brothers and a sister.

But for the sake of the girls, she was willing to try.

Jake watched as Oregon and Joe both bid Breezy farewell. He hadn't meant to make them feel uncomfortable. He hadn't meant to sound like the ruler of clan Martin. Old habits died hard.

"I'm sorry." He moved Rosie to one hip and took Violet from Breezy. He didn't miss the dark shadows under her eyes, a good indication chasing after two little girls had left her exhausted. With Marty home she'd have a break tonight.

"No need to apologize. I should have thought before making additional plans. I just…" She shrugged and looked at the floor. "I've been Joe and Oregon, the person with nowhere to go, no one to spend the holidays with. I've had too many years of spending Christmas with strangers."

"And in a sense, you'll be doing it again this year." His understanding even surprised him.

"In a sense, yes."

"What would you have done for Christmas in Oklahoma?"

She had a faraway look in her eyes. Homesickness? Regret? He wanted to ask, but he also didn't want to take that step, to know too much about what she felt.

"I would have spent it with my sister and her extended family. But this is my family now. The twins are my family."

"We're your family," he offered.

"Right, of course."

He'd had his family around him always. Almost to the point of needing a break from them. She'd had the exact opposite. Curiosity got the better of him.

"Breezy, why did Maria keep running? Why didn't she rent an apartment for the two of you?"

"I didn't realize it when I was younger, but she was afraid the police would find us and take me from her. She wasn't all bad. She was a lonely lady and she'd cared for my mom, cared for us kids. She also didn't know what would happen to me since I was the child without any known family, so she took me and ran. She wasn't emotionally healthy." She looked away from him, not letting him in. "There was so much I didn't understand."

"I'm sorry."

She brought her gaze up. "She loved me. She did her best."

What could he say to that?

"You're defending the woman who took you from your family and kept you from having a home?"

"I know you don't understand."

"Probably not."

Because he was looking at a beautiful, talented woman who hadn't lived the life she should have lived. Senator Brooks might have found her, might have taken care of her. But it was all water under the bridge.

"They're starting to practice." She headed toward the front of the fellowship hall. "And there's Brody."

Jake's younger brother headed their way, wearing a giant-size grin. Violet ran over to him and he picked her up.

"Did the two of you hear that someone bought Cora a van, had it delivered to her little house yesterday along with a trunkload of groceries?" Brody asked when he reached them. The news about the young mom who had eaten Sunday lunch with them came as a surprise.

"I hadn't heard." Jake watched as Breezy drifted away from the two of them. He watched her go and wondered about a woman who had spent her life with nothing but had recently inherited enough for several lifetimes. Was she playing Santa to the poor in Martin's Crossing?

"Yeah, that and the check the church got, and Anna Cranston got a surprise yesterday. That roof of hers has been leaking. Someone must have noticed because a crew showed up to fix it." Brody held both twins now. They were patting his cheeks and pulling at his hat.

Jake glanced from his younger brother to the woman now taking her place at the front of the church. She looked comfortable there in her long skirt, boots and a sweater. She fit in. She glanced his way. He tipped his hat to her and started to walk away. He was at the church for a business meeting, and to help plan the order of events for the Christmas celebration. He wasn't there to watch Breezy.

When he started to turn away, Brody stood in his way.

"You think it's our new sister?" Brody asked, grinning as he rocked back on his boot heels and peered up at Jake.

"She *isn't* our sister," Jake warned.

Brody laughed at that. "No, she isn't, is she? Glad you noticed."

"What are you getting at, Brody?"

"Nothing, don't be so touchy. I wondered if you thought she might be the one playing Santa."

"No, I don't think so." He managed another quick look at the woman in question. "I don't know, maybe."

Brody stood next to Jake, still holding the twins. Violet had his hat on her head. "I'm going to take them to the nursery. But, Jake…"

The tone, serious, a little sad, caught Jake's attention. And he knew. It happened every Christmas. Every year the questions started for Brody. He was the one who had never given up hope that Sylvia Martin would come back. Jake guessed he didn't blame his little brother. Jake had been twelve, but Brody had only been in preschool when she left.

The kid had needed a mom.

"Go ahead, Brody. Ask."

Brody shifted the twins, hugging Violet tightly enough that she protested by wiggling and he set her down. She moved to Jake, holding his legs. He picked her up, wondering if it had been confusing for them, being back in their home with Breezy.

"Don't you ever wonder where she is?" Brody finally asked.

"Yeah, sometimes I do, Brody. She used to write. A few times from Florida, once from New York. The letters stopped a long time ago."

"Do you think she's alive?"

Jake didn't have an answer to that, but he

didn't want his kid brother to have false hope. "I'd say she probably is."

"I've thought about hiring someone to find her."

Jake tamped down his temper. Violet had her head on his shoulder but she looked up at him, big blue eyes questioning and a little worried. He managed to keep his tone soft for her sake. "Brody, why? She didn't want to be a mother twenty-two years ago. I doubt she feels any differently today or she would have come back."

Brody looked like a kid who'd lost his favorite toy. Jake hated that. He didn't want to feel like the guy who kicked the dog. It made him angry all over again. He'd been picking up the pieces for years, and each year at Christmas he picked them up all over again. For Brody. Maybe for Samantha, too.

This year there would be four missing spaces in their lives and at their table. Parents, a sister, a brother-in-law.

He looked over to Breezy and watched as she spoke to Dotty Williams, a sweet old thing with too many cats. Everyone avoided Dotty's pies at church potluck dinners. Those cats were notorious for climbing on counters and inside mixing bowls.

Breezy laughed at something the woman said and then hugged her. Breezy filled up the empty spaces. He was waiting, unwilling to completely trust that she would stay.

He realized that was the difference between himself and Brody. His kid brother kept waiting for a mother who wasn't coming home.

Jake refused to believe that anyone would stay.

# Chapter Eleven

Breezy pulled into the drive long past ten that night. Choir practice had been wonderful. The people of Martin's Crossing had welcomed her into their group, made her feel like a part of things. After parking she sat in her car for a minute. It felt good, to have this town and these people. It felt good to have the twins, as exhausting as they were.

Violet and Rosie had gone home with Brody and Jake. Marty was home and the girls seemed ready to go back to what had become their normal routine at Jake's house.

That meant Breezy was alone again in this house, with the memories she was trying to piece together, and the missing spaces that would never be filled. She reached into the backseat for her purse and, exhausted but happy, climbed out of the car. As she walked up to the front door something stirred in the grass.

She stopped, listening to the softest sound. Maybe it was just a rabbit or a stray cat. She reached into her purse for her keys and raised her hand to unlock the door. She heard it again. The hairs on the back of her neck stood on end. A chill swept through her, setting her nerves on edge.

Wanting her hands free, she put her purse on the chair next to the door and kept her arm bent, ready to take aim at a face if someone sneaked up behind her. As she put the key in the lock she tried to tell herself it had been her imagination. She was used to living in cities and the silence of the country must be getting to her.

Who lived in places this quiet? This dark? She laughed a little at her own apprehension. Of course that's all it was. The wind had rustled the shrubs and she'd panicked. She pushed the door open and reached for the alarm system, then thought better of it. She had a minute to punch in the code. A minute to make sure she was alone, that there wasn't really someone out there.

As she reached back to get her purse, the body came at her from the dark end of the porch. He shoved before she could prepare herself. She fell back against the door and tried to steady herself.

"I'm not going down without a fight!" she yelled. As she went at the man, pushing her palm into his nose and then kicking him in the gut, he fought back, knocking her sideways. Her head hit the wall and her legs crumpled.

The alarm went off, screeching into the night air, breaking that country stillness with a vengeance. Her attacker ran for the back office. Breezy grabbed her purse and found the pepper spray. But as she ran through the house, she heard the back door slam. He was gone.

The house phone rang. She picked it up, answering the call from the alarm company. They asked her if she was okay. She told them she needed the police. No, she didn't need an ambulance. And then she sank back to the floor.

Headlights flashed before blue lights. She pushed herself to her feet and walked to the door with her head pounding, feeling less than steady on her feet. Jake jumped out of his truck. Behind him another truck pulled up. Duke got out, racing his brother to the house.

Martins to the rescue, she thought. She giggled, but that hurt, too. She pushed her fingers against her temple and winced.

"What happened?" Jake shouted as he headed up the sidewalk.

She shook her head only slightly. "Could you not yell?"

"Is he still here?" Jake continued.

Duke had joined them. "Maybe give her a minute?"

Jake took a deep breath and Breezy shot Duke a grateful look. "Thank you. No, he ran out the back door. He was waiting for me to open the door and deactivate the alarm, I think. Good thing I heard something and decided to not deactivate the alarm."

Duke grinned at that. "Good thinking, sis."

Jake came closer than was necessary. Or at least that's what Breezy thought. She closed her eyes and his fingers brushed her temple, pushing her hair back and then settling on the knot that had come up on the side of her head.

"That should probably be checked out."

"I'm fine, just a little loopy from getting pushed into a wall."

"Right, of course you're fine. But we'll still get that checked."

"At the Martin's Crossing E.R.?" she teased.

"No, we'll have to take a drive to Austin."

"I'm not interested," she argued. But her vision wavered a little. "But I would like to sit down."

Jake picked her up. It happened in one swoop. His arm was around her shoulder one minute and the next his other arm swept beneath her knees. "I can walk. I..."

"You want to keep arguing until you pass out?" He grinned in the dim light of the porch. "Relax."

They walked inside. Or Jake and Duke walked. Breezy allowed herself to be carried, to be the damsel in distress, just once. She told herself she wouldn't do it again. She'd been taking care of herself a long time. And it wasn't the first time she'd been on the receiving end of a man's fist. But it felt good to be in his arms. It felt safe there. Why wouldn't she rest her head on his shoulder, breathe in his scent? Any woman in her position would.

She might have suffered a concussion but she hadn't been knocked senseless. She sighed as she relaxed in his arms.

Outside the window, blue lights flashed and a siren wailed. Duke took a careful look around the house as Jake settled her on the sofa. He reached for the afghan on the back of the rocking chair and covered her with it.

"I really don't need a blanket."

"Of course you do." He tucked it up to her chin.

"I'm really okay."

"Yeah, I know you are. But humor me."

Duke reappeared with a bag of frozen corn.

He handed it to Jake, who settled it on the side of her head. She flinched as the cold touched her skin.

"You should see the other guy." She teased, even though her head did ache.

He laughed a little. "I bet. Did you manage to get a good shot when you hit him? And did you see his face?"

"I think I probably broke his nose." She grinned up at the cowboy leaning over her, his blue eyes searching her as if looking for other signs of injury. "And no, I didn't see his face."

She told herself not to be too overcome by his hero act. He took care of everyone. He would have done this for a stranger.

Commotion at the front door ended the conversation and her rush of emotions. Duke spoke to the officers and led them inside. One took off through the house, the other approached her.

"Do you need an ambulance?" he asked as he stood over her. Why did the cops always look imposing, even when they were on her side? She shivered a little and shook her head.

"I'm good."

He asked questions then, about the suspect, about his build, any identifying traits, if she'd seen a vehicle. The only thing she knew was that he had been about her height and he probably had a broken nose. The officer smiled at that and wrote information on the tablet he'd carried in with him.

The other officer returned. "There's some blood in the kitchen."

"From the broken nose." Jake laughed as he said it.

They discussed evidence. The door to the office had been opened but because the alarm had gone off the guy had left, running out the back door.

"He could have had a gun." Jake pulled a chair close to the sofa.

Breezy opened her eyes and looked up at him. "But he didn't. Or if he did, he wasn't interested in shooting me. He's looking for something."

"Right, and he was willing to slam you against a wall."

"Jake, I'm fine."

As she said the words she knew that she wasn't fine. Not really. Maybe she would be physically, but emotionally she knew she had a real problem. For the first time in her life, she wanted to be taken care of. She wanted to be protected by this man, held in his arms.

And that scared her. More than the intruder ever had.

The deputies finished their investigating and told Jake that unfortunately they couldn't find much to go on. He walked them out, then returned to the living room, where a medic from the local first-responder unit was examining Breezy. He'd insisted it was either the local guys or he would take her to Austin.

Duke had left. Jake thought it would be a good idea for one of them to be at the Circle M, just in case their prowler thought he might find what he was looking for in Jake's office.

"How is she?" Jake asked the medic as he sat down on the edge of a chair. Breezy touched the knot on her head, wincing. He guessed that was his answer.

The medic, a guy who had been in Afghanistan twice in the past few years, gave her one last look. "I think she's okay. She said she never lost consciousness. I do think it would be a good idea for her to stay awake for several hours. If the headache changes, speech slurs, you know the symptoms to watch for."

Jake did know the symptoms. Brody had been riding bulls for ten years. They were concussion experts.

"We can handle it. She'll be at my house where Marty and I can keep an eye on her."

"I can stay here!"

"Of course you would argue." He leaned back, watching as the medic packed up his stuff. Boone was a good guy. He'd grown up on a ranch outside of town, and his folks had gone through some tough times.

"Ma'am, no arguing with this," Boone said. "You really have to be with people tonight. And you have no idea who this guy is and if he'll come back."

She looked around the house, now lit with overhead lighting. Jake watched as her gaze landed on the nativity she'd put on the mantel and then the tree. He'd told her to make this house her own, add her stuff. And she had.

He thought he understood her reluctance. "It's a day, two at the most, Breezy."

She nodded and moved to the edge of the sofa. "I need to pack a bag."

"I can help," he offered.

A smile broke across her face. "No, you can't. But thank you."

A few minutes later, they were heading down the road to the Circle M. He shot a cautious look at the woman in the truck next to him. The light was dim and he couldn't make out her expression, but he heard her weary sigh, saw her lean a little toward the window as she clutched her overnight bag in her lap.

"You okay?"

"I'm good. I just thought it would be different here. It isn't supposed to be like this."

"Care to share?"

She shook her head. "No, not really."

He pulled up to his house, easing the truck into the garage. Duke's truck was parked out front in the circle drive. He had caught sight of his brother sitting on the front porch in the cold. Jake guessed he wasn't the only one with the burden of needing to protect.

They walked in through the garage door that led through a utility room, a breakfast room and then the kitchen. The giant-size kitchen that the woman who had agreed to marry him insisted she would need. Only she hadn't really wanted a kitchen in a ranch house in Texas Hill Country. She was now married to a doctor in Austin. Jake hadn't quite met her standards.

The same way his dad hadn't met Sylvia's standards. She'd wanted to be a socialite, not a rancher's wife.

He shrugged it off. "Want a cup of coffee? I can plug in the Keurig."

She sat down on a bar stool, dropping her bag on the floor next to her. "Sure, if I have to stay awake, I might as well have coffee."

The machine was already plugged in and the water reservoir filled. Marty must have anticipated they'd need it. From the living room he heard the door click and then the alarm system computer voice said, "Alarm activated."

Duke walked into the room a few minutes later. "Coffee?"

"Yes. I guess you want a cup." Jake pulled three cups out of the cabinet.

"Might as well if we're going to be up all night."

Breezy spun on the chair to face him. "You don't have to stay up. I'm really okay."

Duke took off his hat and tossed it on the counter. "Listen, sis, none of us is going anywhere. That's how we Martins roll. We stick together."

"I'm not a…"

He patted her hand, silencing her. "Yeah, you're one of us. So relax. Let Jake take care of you or he'll break out in hives."

"Jake has enough on his plate without the burden of me. I don't think that's my reason for being in Martin's Crossing."

"Oh, I think it is." Duke headed around the counter to make his own cup of coffee. Jake shot him a lethal glare.

"What's going on?"

Jake pushed a cup under the spout of the Keurig. "Nothing. How do you like your coffee?"

"Since I don't drink coffee, I'll take it however you think is best."

"Cream and sugar," Duke offered. Jake shot

him another look. "What did I do now? You know, I think I'll head to the living room and put my feet up."

"Good idea." Jake spooned sugar into the cup and added cream. He set it in front of Breezy. She rested her elbows on the counter and laced her fingers together to rest her chin on her hands. He thought she looked done in, and guessed by morning they'd all look a little worse for wear.

"Thank you." She pulled the coffee to her and raised it to take a sip. Her eyes closed and she sighed. "Why haven't I ever been a coffee drinker?"

"Maybe you haven't had the right coffee?"

"Could be."

Jake made his coffee and sat down next to her. "Breezy, what happened?"

"A guy broke into my house."

He sighed and placed a hand over hers. "In California. On the streets."

"Oh, that."

Pain flashed across her features. Sadness and anger followed.

"Yeah, that. You said you thought it would be different here. I want to make sure it's different."

He wanted to give her a home that no one took from her, a place filled with family and friends. He couldn't stop thinking about the sister they'd taken her away from. Or Lawton had taken her from. He knew she'd wanted to stay in Oklahoma and build that relationship.

"You're very sweet, Jake." She moved her hand, turning it so that their hands were palm to palm, and then she laced her fingers through his and brought his hand to her lips, kissing his knuckles.

"And you won't tell me?"

She shrugged slim shoulders beneath the sweatshirt she'd changed into before leaving. "There isn't a lot to tell. We moved from town to town. My social life was rather nonexistent. It wasn't as if I dated, went to a prom or hung out with friends. And there were times along the way that men thought, because of our situation, that I, that I…"

He wouldn't make her say it. "You deserve better."

She released his hand. "Most people do. I'm really okay, Jake. Tonight took me by surprise, that's all."

"I think it took us all by surprise. In a day or two, as soon as I know we're safe here, I'm going to take a trip to Austin and talk to some of the employees at Lawton's company."

"Should I go? I mean, what if it's one of them and I need to identify someone?"

"I think we'll know him by his broken nose."

She laughed the slightest bit and then they finished their coffee in silence.

Sometime close to dawn he allowed her to go to sleep. She curled up on the sofa and in minutes she was out. Jake watched her as she succumbed to sleep and then he stood to leave. He had chores that wouldn't wait. Marty was standing in the doorway. She didn't say anything. Better for him to pretend she hadn't been watching with those eagle eyes of hers.

"I'm going to get some work done, and make sure the guys know what needs to be done today." He marched toward the back of the house.

"Is that all you're going to say?"

"Nothing else to say." He grabbed his jacket off the hook by the back door. "And I already know you want to say something. Please don't."

He was thirty-four years old. He didn't need to have his housekeeper tell him what he was feeling.

If she didn't say anything, he could keep telling himself that Breezy was one more person he needed to take care of and nothing more. Then he wouldn't have to admit to himself that he *wanted* to take care of her.

# Chapter Twelve

Breezy somehow slept for hours on the sofa in Jake's living room. She slept through the twins poking at her face, Duke arguing with Brody and Jake going to town to order grain. She knew all of this because Marty told her.

The two of them were in the kitchen going through recipes when Jake walked through the back door. She looked up from the notebook she was using to copy recipes and made cautious eye contact with the man walking through the kitchen. His mouth eased into a smile.

Marty cleared her throat and pushed an index card across the counter. "What about this one for gumbo?"

Breezy looked at the recipe. "Sounds great. Have you made it?"

Marty nodded and looked a little teary. "I used to make it twice a month on Fridays. Earl and I would have friends over for dinner to play games and I'd make the gumbo. One of our friends would bake bread. Those were wonderful times."

"Then I definitely want this recipe."

"And here's one for pizza crust that's so easy." Marty pushed that card to her, as well.

"Thank you. This means so much to me, Marty."

"I'm glad to do it. We never had children so it means a lot to me that someone will be using these and passing them down."

Breezy glanced over her shoulder to check on the twins. They were being very quiet. They had plastic bowls, lids and spoons that Marty had given them to play with. Sometimes the bowls were musical instruments, sometimes they pretended to cook.

Violet turned a bowl over and pounded on it and Rosie tried to take the spoon. A squabble ensued. Breezy started to hop down off the stool but Marty put a hand on her arm, stopping her.

"Give them a minute. They aren't pulling hair or biting, so they might work it out," the older woman advised.

It wasn't easy to sit back and watch. But eventually Rosie gave up on the spoon. Big tears welled in her blue eyes and she stood and toddled to Breezy. As Breezy reached to pick her up, Rosie sobbed a little. "Mama."

Breezy held the child close, patting her back. "Aunt Breezy, honey."

Marty shook her head. "Mama is who you are, Breezy."

"No, they have, they…" She buried her face in Rosie's dark hair, inhaling the lavender and chamomile scent of her baby shampoo.

Marty rubbed Breezy's back much the way she rubbed Rosie's. "They have you. They have Jake and of course they have all of us."

"I don't know how to do this, Marty. I'm not prepared."

"You're doing it, though. Maybe you weren't prepared. We hardly ever are prepared for life's challenges. But we manage. I think if we knew the challenges were coming, instead of taking them on, we'd run."

Violet had pushed aside her bowl and spoon and joined them. Marty pulled her to her lap. That's how Jake found the four of them. Breezy wiped her eyes with her hand as he walked back into the room, his expression puzzled.

"From recipes to tears. What are you two doing?"

Breezy chuckled a little, the sound mixing with a sob. "We just had a moment."

Marty pointed at Breezy. "Mama."

Jake's smile faded. Breezy wanted to say something, to stop him from walking away. She didn't want to take his sister's place, to replace her.

"Jake," Marty called to him as he walked away.

"Just give me a minute," he called back.

"I should say something." Breezy started to get up. Again, Marty stopped her.

"One thing you learn is that when a Martin says he needs a minute, you give him a minute. He and Elizabeth were close, Breezy. They practically raised this family. They cooked. They kept things clean. They kept their dad functioning and sometimes kept him off the drink. Losing Elizabeth was like losing a part of himself."

He took care of everyone else. So who took care of Jake?

She heard the front door close.

Marty took Rosie from her. "You go. I've got these two. He'll be in the barn. But don't be surprised if he runs you off."

"I'm not easily frightened."

Marty grinned at that. "And that's why he needs you."

Jake needed her. She shook her head at the thought. Jake didn't seem to need anyone. But something small inside her had ignited and she wanted to be the person he needed, the person who was there for him.

She hurried out the back door, grabbing her coat as she went. She hadn't been to the barns on the Circle M. There were several. There was an old barn in the field behind the house. It was wood-sided, gray and weathered with a new metal roof and obvious repairs. To the west of the house was a metal structure. It housed equipment and hay. And then there was a metal building with wide doors that pushed open and a standard door to the side of that. Horses grazed in the field to the right of the barn. In the distance a tractor hauled a big round bale of hay to cattle. She picked this as the right barn.

She didn't know what she would say to Jake but she knew that it was time he let someone be there for him.

The barn was lit with overhead lights down the center of the tall ceiling. On one side were half a dozen stalls. On the side were various doors. She called out for Jake but he didn't answer. She knocked on the first door and got no reply. She opened the door to find a feed room and tack room. The next room held trophies and saddles.

And then she heard a pounding sound and the sound of feet scuffing the earth. She started to knock on the door but knew he wouldn't answer.

She turned the knob and opened the door slowly, peeking in as she did.

Jake stood in the center of the room. No, he wasn't standing. He was boxing. The room was a gym. There were weights, a treadmill, a television, chairs and the boxing bag on a stand in the center of the room. He jabbed at it, letting it come back to him and then jabbing again. As she watched, he went at it, pounding hard with both fists.

He was breathing heavily and in the noise she heard his sobs. She should go, let him grieve in piece. But how could she walk away? How could she let this be one more thing that Jake Martin seemed to do on his own?

As she stood in the doorway contemplating her next move, he spotted her and shook his head.

"Go away," he said in a quiet voice that rumbled like thunder through a stormy night.

She shook her head. He was stubborn. She could show him she was just as stubborn, if not more so. He needed her, whether he wanted to admit it or not. Maybe that's what had brought the two of them together.

Maybe God had known she needed a place of her own and He'd known that Jake Martin needed someone strong enough to stand toe to toe with him, strong enough to be there for him.

He reached for a towel, wiping it across his face before wrapping it around his neck. She closed the distance between them. As she reached for him, he pulled her hard against him, holding her tight.

Jake hadn't expected her. He hadn't expected her to search him out. He hadn't expected to need her. He'd come to the barn thinking he'd do what he always did. He'd box. Maybe he'd go for a ride. He'd think, figure it out, move on. But the pain had followed him, pounding against him as he'd pounded that punching bag.

It was relentless, wave after wave of grief.

Breezy's arms were around him as he held her tight against him, soaking up the comfort in her embrace, in the words she whispered. He didn't really hear them, but they were there, pouring over him like summer rain.

He pulled her head to his shoulder and kissed her brow. Man, he needed this woman. For how long, though? How long would she be here, soaking up his pain, his grief? How long would she be here to make him smile when only weeks ago he'd wondered if any of them would ever be happy again?

"You can lean on people, Jake." The words were muffled against his shoulder, her warm breath permeating his shirt. He stroked his hand down the softness of her hair, thinking through the words that she spoke as if they made perfect sense.

What did he say to that? How did he lean on people? If he leaned on someone, how did he stay strong? He hadn't leaned on anyone since… never? Maybe he'd leaned on Elizabeth. Sometimes, every now and then, he leaned on Duke. But Duke joined the army at twenty-one and for eight years he'd been gone.

A long time ago, the day their mother left, Jake tried to lean on his dad. But Gabe Martin had pushed him away, told him to figure out how to turn on the oven if they were hungry. If they were out of groceries, he told him to drive to town but don't get caught.

Elizabeth had been a mess, the same age as him but needing a mom. Duke had been angry and had rode off on his horse. Brody had been about four and still trying to run from the house to chase Sylvia down. Samantha had been little more than a baby.

The grief had finally left their dad but he hadn't been there to lean on. Ever.

When he didn't answer Breezy, she looked up at him, for all the world looking like she had meant her words of comfort.

"You can at least lean on me," she said with

conviction. "We're parents together. That's what parents do."

He brushed a kiss across her cheek and sighed. "Yeah. Parents."

And parents were called Mom and Dad. It was natural for the twins to begin to see her as mom, him as dad. He thought that in time they would need that connection. Look at Brody, a kid who'd never had a mom. He was still looking for her.

"Thank you." He finally croaked out the words.

"Do you have water in that fridge over there?" She nodded toward the fridge at the far side of the room.

"Yeah." He pulled her with him to open it and grabbed two bottles.

"Is this where you go when you're upset?"

He looked around the room. It had started with a punching bag and he'd built it into this. "Yes, this is where I go."

"Try going to a friend once in a while."

She smiled up at him and he felt like a puzzle with the pieces coming together. He brushed a hand across her cheek, tangling his fingers in the silky strands of blond hair. With caramel eyes, melting, darkening, she looked up at him. He leaned, tilting his head to find the right angle as he closed his lips over hers.

She kissed him back, her free hand going to the nape of his neck, sliding into his hair. He tried not to need people.

He couldn't lie about needing her. He needed to pour his hurt into her and have her hold him until it started to heal. He brushed his hand up her back and she stood on tiptoe, her lips soft beneath his.

He eventually pulled back. He had a lot of questions about himself, about her, about the future. They'd have to figure out the answers. Because Lawton had planned this. He'd told Jake when he mentioned making the two of them guardians that he thought they'd both be single, even twenty years from now. Single and lonely, waiting for the right person to come into their lives, so they'd make the perfect guardians for the twins.

Lawton hadn't meant to leave them now. Jake leaned back into the woman standing close to him. Her arms circled his neck and she placed a kiss against his chin.

"Let's go for a ride," he suggested, amused when her eyes widened.

"Ride? In your truck, you mean?"

"Horses. Come on. It's warm and there's no rain."

She was his rain. He needed to soak her up like the land after a long drought. For today, maybe just for the moment, he needed her close. Later he'd figure out what to do with these feelings.

She pulled back on his hand as he tried to tug her toward the door. "I've never ridden a horse."

"You live in Texas. It's time to learn."

How long had it been since he'd flirted with a woman? Or even let down his guard long enough to enjoy being around a woman? How long since he'd taken a few minutes to relax, to not worry about who was taking care of things? He needed this. And she must have realized because she allowed him to lead her through the barn.

"I'm not sure if this is a good idea," she said as she stood in the doorway that led to the corral.

He winked. "You'll do great. I'll be right back."

With two lead ropes he trudged through the corral to the gate. He whistled and the horses looked up, ears twitching as they watched him. He shook a bucket of grain and that got their attention. The small herd, just five of them, headed his way. He opened the gate and culled the two they would ride. A big chestnut he'd been riding lately and a small bay gelding for Breezy.

After the horses were saddled he led her to

the corral and helped her up. She put her left foot in the stirrup and swung her right leg over, landing with a thud in the saddle. She looked down at him, unsure, unsteady but with a definite spark of adventure in her eyes.

"You'll do great with Montego."

"Montego?" She brushed her hand down the horse's neck, still looking more than a little nervous.

"Bay." He grinned. "Montego Bay."

He gave her a short riding lesson and then he swung himself into his saddle and rode up next to her. He'd closed the gate to the field and opened the gate leading out of the corral. There were plenty of back trails, and with some daylight left they'd have a good ride.

"Where are we going?" She rode next to him and he had to give her credit, she didn't look like it was her first time in the saddle. She had a natural ease, holding the reins lightly, her heels down and her legs relaxed.

But he could see the slight tremble in her hands, the occasional clenching of her jaw.

"Not far." He nodded toward the hills in the distance, a half mile back. "There's a pretty stream at the base of those hills. Sometimes there's a deer or two, so don't get too relaxed and drop your reins. If you horse starts, go with the motion and keep a firm hand."

Her eyes widened. "Will he startle? I thought he was gentle."

"He's as gentle as they come, but any horse can startle. Get used to the feel of him. Even with a saddle you'll feel him tense. Right now you can feel that he's relaxed."

She rode for a few paces and nodded. "Okay, I've got this."

"That's good. Never think you've got this. Be confident, but always expect the unexpected."

*Expect the unexpected.* She was the unexpected and she'd sure caught him off guard. He'd expected her to take the money and run, not be tied down to two little girls she didn't know.

He hadn't expected her to be all-in the way she'd proven to be. She'd even made herself at home in Martin's Crossing.

But these weren't the thoughts he wanted to go over again. He needed to clear his head. He eased a look in her direction and shook his head. Yeah, he needed to get it together. Because he was thinking of kissing her again. That couldn't happen.

If he complicated their relationship this way, how would they manage to go on, raising the girls together? He hadn't thought of that before, because for two weeks he'd been trying to figure out how to manage being parents together.

He'd been trying to figure out how to trust her in their lives and trust that she wouldn't leave.

Now he had to face that they were in a situation that required them to be more than parents. They were in each other's lives. Day in, day out, counting on each other, turning to each other. It was a given that someday one, or both, of them would want to settle down, get married. To someone else.

But this relationship, allowing it to become a flirtation, or even casual dating, that would only end in disaster. Because if it ended, they would still have to face each other every day and still be the best parents they could be to the twins.

Kissing her again was the last thing he should be thinking about.

After the ride Breezy sat on the step to the tack room and watched as Jake unsaddled and brushed the horses. He'd insisted she should watch this time, and next time he'd let her help. So she watched, because who wouldn't want to watch a cowboy in faded jeans that fit just right brush a horse? She watched as he lifted hooves and cleaned them with a pick. She watched as he untied first one horse and then the other and led them to the gate.

"You're quiet," he said when he returned. He

reached for the jacket he'd left on a hook and tossed it to her. "It's getting cold."

"Thank you. I was just thinking that I feel okay and I'll probably go back to Lawton's."

"There's no reason you can't stay here," he said, holding out a hand and helping her to her feet.

"I know, but my stuff is at Lawton's. And I can't run in fear."

They walked out of the barn. He flipped off the lights as they left. He'd been right, the air was colder. The sky was steel-gray, no evidence of the setting sun. She shivered in the warmth of a jacket that smelled like Jake.

"You have to start calling it your place, Breezy," he said quietly as they walked. The dog had joined them and it raced ahead, chasing something, then came back.

"Easier said than done."

"Yeah, I know. I think we're both having a hard time taking possession. Of the twins, the house..." He paused.

She filled in the empty space. "Lawton and Elizabeth's life."

He only nodded, his gaze faraway. An arm went around her waist, pulling her close to his side. "You don't think it's Joe, do you?"

She shook her head. "Too tall."

"Good."

They walked in silence and Breezy knew she was in trouble. She knew the comfort from his arm around her waist was trouble. It anchored her in a way that a plant, a nativity, an ornament only hinted at. It made her feel as if she had found a home, and it was in Jake Martin's arms.

That was when she knew that she really had to make her escape back to Lawton's.

## Chapter Thirteen

Breezy went home the next day, and life slipped back into an easy routine. During the day the girls were often with her, and in the evening they went back to the Circle M. Jake sometimes stayed around while they were with her. He would work outside and then they would eat dinner together in the evenings before he took the girls home.

Breezy poured through the recipes Marty had given her. She made casseroles, soups, breads and anything else she thought Jake and two little girls would eat. And they did.

Christmas was a little over a week away and she had shopped in town, finding gifts that she wrapped and put under the tree. She had shopped at the antique store and found small things to put around the house to make it feel like her home. A braided rug for the kitchen, a picture in her bedroom, a pretty clock for the living room.

She and Jake had developed an easy friendship. And wasn't that what they needed in order to raise two little girls? It should have been one of their first rules, to be friends. But their friendship could easily get blurred around the edges because, even as their friendship grew, Breezy remembered how it felt to be held by him. And every now and then when they stood too close or accidentally touched, she knew that he felt it, too. It was an indrawn breath, a moment of stillness, a certain connection when their eyes met.

But another rule seemed to be that they not mention that attraction for fear that it would undo their friendship.

On a cold Friday night they met in town for the annual Christmas block party. The stores were open late. Duke was serving hot drinks and pie. A few vendors had set up around the park, in tribute to their German ancestors selling handmade toys and crafts, brats and other treats. The Christmas lights were lit up and each building was decorated.

Breezy found Jake at a vendor buying bratwursts for him and fries for the girls. He had them in a stroller built for two. From several feet away she watched as he pulled off his gloves to pay for the food. He tested a fry before handing them to the girls.

He must have sensed that she was there because he nodded at her. She greeted the twins first. It was easier. It gave her heart time to calm down, to realize she wanted what she couldn't have. Hadn't she learned that it could only lead to a world of hurt?

She squatted in front of the stroller, kissing first Rosie and then Violet. "You girls look perfect tonight, like cotton candy."

They were dressed in puffy pink coats, pink stocking caps and pink gloves. Their jeans were tucked into pink-and-brown boots.

"Candy!" Rosie shoved a fry in her mouth.

"Too big a bite, little girl." Breezy opened her hand and Rosie gave her a look and kept chewing. "Okay, but small bites."

Rosie took another fry and bit a small piece off the end. "Small bites."

"Bites." Violet giggled.

"Do you want a brat?" Jake asked.

She stood and turned to the vendor. He was looking past them at people starting to form a line. "Yes, that would be good."

While they waited, she pushed the girls' stroller to the side, making room for the crowds that were starting to form. It surprised her, to see so many people in this little town. There were people admiring the lights, people walking in and out of shops.

Jake handed her the brat and then his gaze slid past her. She looked in the same direction, not sure what he saw. There were people. Few of them were familiar to her. She saw Joe walking in the crowd, talking to a member of the church. Farther in the distance she saw Brody walking with a young woman.

"I'm sorry. Can I leave the twins with you for a minute?"

Breezy shrugged as she finished a bite of brat. "Sure. Is something wrong?"

"Tyler Randall is here. He's the man in charge of Lawton's company. I'm surprised to see him here."

"Go ahead. We'll wander around. I'm sure we'll find stuff we want."

He grinned at that, then he leaned a little closer. For a second she thought he might kiss her. Instead he brushed his finger across her cheek. "Mustard."

"Oh." She managed a smile and then she watched as he walked away, her heart beating a million miles an hour.

After finishing her brat, she pushed the stroller down the sidewalk, admiring local arts and crafts. She stopped at a lighted tent filled with handmade wooden toys. A rocking horse caught her eye. Two rocking horses. They couldn't have just one or there would be fights.

As she admired the horses, Oregon entered the tent. The other woman joined her. "They're precious."

"Yes, I think they would make perfect Christmas gifts for the twins." She flipped the price tag and was surprised by a price much lower than she would have expected.

"How are things going?" Oregon asked as she looked at painted wall plaques.

"Good. I'm still learning but I think we're managing," Breezy answered as she waved to the vendor and pointed to the two rocking horses.

"You'll always be learning. Lilly is almost twelve and I'm always one step ahead of her or two steps behind."

"So you're telling me it doesn't get easier?"

Oregon shrugged "There are easier moments."

"How's your shop doing?" Breezy listened to the man tell her the price of the horses and she pulled out her wallet. "Aren't you open tonight?"

"I am. I wanted to take a few minutes to browse so Joe is watching the shop."

Breezy paid for the horses and asked the vendor to hold them for her until she could arrange free hands to carry them to her car. She and Oregon walked out of the shop together.

They were strolling toward a hot apple cider stand. Oregon stopped walking, her hand on Breezy's arm to bring her to a halt.

"What's up?" Breezy pulled the stroller back so she was closer to her friend. Oregon glanced around, her bottom lip between her teeth. "Oregon?"

"Someone bought my building."

"They did what? Are they going to make you move out?"

"No, they bought it and signed the deed over to me," Oregon explained.

"Who?" Breezy looked around to make sure they weren't attracting attention. Fortunately they'd found a somewhat quiet spot. In the distance a small group stood on a corner caroling. A car honked and someone laughed. But she and Oregon were alone.

"I'm not sure. A lawyer showed up the other day and told me the building had been bought and that I was the new owner. I'm not sure what to think."

"I think you've been given a wonderful opportunity. Now you don't have to worry as much about the winter slowdown after Christmas." Breezy knew that had been on Oregon's mind. She had some internet business from her website, but from what Oregon had told her, it wouldn't have been enough to cover expenses.

"Yes, a great opportunity. But who does something like that? Who gives a young mom a new van, a church a five-figure check and me a building?"

"Someone with a big heart and a lot of money?"

Oregon was looking at her, dark eyes suspicious. "Some people think it might be you."

Breezy laughed. "It isn't me. Not that I don't consider myself bighearted, but I'm barely registering my new circumstances enough to allow myself to write a check for groceries."

They started walking again, the hot cider luring them in.

"I'm really thankful," Oregon said, her voice soft. "But I'm also suspicious."

"Don't be. Whoever is doing this is obviously trying to help people at Christmastime. I think that's what Christmas is all about. I know that there were a lot of years when I wouldn't have had Christmas, period, if someone hadn't donated money."

"It must have been tough," Oregon said.

Tough. Yes, she guessed it had. It had been tough. And frightening at times.

"It was tough," she agreed. "But it wasn't always bad. Maria usually found a way to get us a room, usually efficiency apartments. She made sure I studied. She would find school books at used book stores. She made sure I got my GED."

They bought hot apple cider and headed for the light display. There were lights in the shape of the nativity, the wise men and a star that stood on a tower above the entire display. There were camels that seemed to move, shepherds in a field and angels singing.

If everything continued to go well she would live here for a long time. She would visit this park every Christmas, and shop in these same stores where people knew her name.

She stood listening to the carolers on the sidewalk in front of the church and she realized that most importantly she seemed to have found herself here in Martin's Crossing. She had found a home. A place to belong.

The star, dozens of feet up in the air, twinkled in the night as snow flurries drifted down. They were big flakes, the kind that didn't last long, but looked so beautiful as they fell.

The most important thing, she realized, was faith. Because in this town of traditions she had finally realized that God loved even her. She'd always wanted to believe, to have faith, but she'd wondered if God even knew she existed. Sometimes in life she had felt that invisible.

He not only knew she existed, but He cared.

The choir sang "Joy to the World." Oregon

sang along. Breezy joined her. The snow continued to fall and a crowd gathered with everyone singing together. Breezy looked around. Vendors had stepped out of their shops. The crowds had stopped walking.

The snow fell a little harder. Breezy pulled the top out on the stroller so that the twins were protected and found blankets to tuck around them.

This is how home felt. And she smiled.

Jake could hear the carolers but he couldn't get away to join Breezy and the twins. He studied Tyler Randall's face and wondered if he trusted the man.

"Anyway, Jake, things are going well. I'm hoping for a government contract on that new software."

"Sounds good, Tyler. You've always known how to bring these deals together. If you need my help, let me know."

"I think I've got it."

He still didn't get what Tyler was doing in Martin's Crossing. The story Tyler told him was that he'd heard Lawton talk about this festival and he'd wanted to see it for himself. There were a lot of Christmas festivals he could have attended. Most were bigger. And definitely closer to Austin.

"Where's the heir apparent?" Tyler asked just as Jake was thinking to make his excuses and walk away.

"Heir apparent?"

"The senator's daughter." Tyler grinned, even winked. Jake couldn't quite push down his dislike of the man.

"Tyler, I'm not sure what's going on with you, but she's Lawton's sister and she deserves respect."

"Oh, so Lawton got his way?"

"What does that mean?"

"Lawton thought two lonely people deserved each other. I guess he hadn't planned on bringing you together this soon in this way."

"He was my best friend, Tyler. And Elizabeth was my sister. We lost a big part of our family in that plane crash. I'm not sure I see the joke in all of this."

"I think you're being overly sensitive," Tyler pushed, still smiling.

Some people just didn't know when to quit.

"Tyler, you might want to remember that I own a portion of this company. That makes me your boss."

Tyler's hands went up in surrender. "Right, gotcha."

"And now, if you don't mind, I have two little girls that I'm supposed to be spending time with."

He walked away because that seemed the safest thing to do. He wasn't sure what would happen if Tyler said anything else that rubbed him the wrong way.

It took him a few minutes but he spotted Breezy and the twins. Snow had begun to fall and they were standing a short distance away from the carolers. They were silhouettes with the lights of the nativity behind them.

He paused to watch as Breezy leaned down, giving sips of her drink to the girls. She tucked their blankets a little closer. When she stood she looked over at him. He waved. She raised a gloved hand and said something to Violet and Rosie. The twins laughed and waved, but not really in his direction.

The music ended. He walked up to Breezy, greeting the twins first. "I'm sorry I got tied up."

"Is everything okay?" Breezy asked as they started walking.

He wasn't sure. But he didn't want to ruin the moment with snow falling and lights twinkling around them.

"Do you want anything else?" he asked.

Breezy shook her head. "No, I just thought we'd walk along the path and look at lights. I take it you don't get a lot of snow here?"

"Very little. This is perfect, though. It isn't freezing cold and this won't amount to much."

"It is perfect."

They walked through the light display with the twins pointing and jabbering. By the time they reached the sidewalk and turned back toward Main Street, the girls were asleep and the crowds had thinned out.

Jake saw Joe walking down a sidewalk away from the shops. He wondered where the old guy went. He guessed everyone was wondering. As he considered what he should do, he saw Duke come out of the restaurant and call Joe over. Duke wouldn't let him sleep on the streets.

"I don't want you to stay at the house alone tonight," Jake finally admitted as they got to her car. That had been on his mind since his meeting with Tyler. He just hadn't known how to bring it up.

"Why?"

He took the keys from her hand and opened her door. "Because I'm not sure why Tyler Randall is in town and I don't trust him."

"Tyler?"

"The employee that I spoke to earlier."

"Oh, right." Breezy tossed her purse in her car. "I have to pull over to one of the vendors and get the rocking horses I bought the twins."

He smiled at that. "They'll love to have those under the tree on Christmas morning."

He watched her go somewhere, drifting on distant memories, he imagined.

"I think they will." She shoved her hands in her pockets. "I really will be okay at the house, Jake."

"I know you will. I know you can take care of yourself. I would appreciate, though, if you would do this for me." He leaned in close. "Because I don't want anything to happen to you."

Her lips parted just slightly and he knew she planned on arguing. Of course she would argue. And he couldn't let her. Not this time. He had a hinky feeling about Tyler. A man with a good dose of greed and jealousy might be willing to do anything to get what he wanted. And Jake was pretty sure Tyler was the man they were searching for.

Before she could say anything he brushed a hand across her cheek and settled it on her neck to pull her to him. He lowered his lips to hers, knowing he shouldn't but unable to resist. Her lips tasted like cherry lip balm and apple cider. He closed his eyes, lingering in a kiss that could have gone on forever.

What was it about this woman?

He brushed his lips across her cheek, heard her sigh as she leaned close, moving to rest her head on his shoulder. He wanted to know that she would stay, not just for the twins, but for him.

He wanted to trust her.

The rangy kid who had watched his mother leave town had a hard time with trust. And that kid was still buried deep inside him, warning him not to get too close.

## Chapter Fourteen

Three days later, both twins had a cold. Their noses were runny and their eyes were watery. Breezy, still at the Circle M until Jake decided her house was safe, sat in the recliner with them, rocking gently. Jake had gone to Austin the previous day. He had shopping to do and business to take care of, he'd said. She thought it more likely that he was digging around, trying to learn if Lawton had been working on something new that he hadn't known about.

As much as Breezy wanted to go back to her own place, she enjoyed the extra time with the twins. She loved holding them, cuddling them against her. She loved when they woke up in the morning and before breakfast they wanted to sit quietly and watch their favorite cartoon. And it broke her heart when every now and then one of them called her Mommy. Marty had told her it would happen. It had to happen.

No one was being disloyal to Lawton and Elizabeth. The twins were babies who needed that connection with a mommy and daddy. It was only natural, Marty had said. Breezy kissed first Violet and then Rosie on the top of the head. Rosie reached up and patted her cheek.

"I need to ask Marty what to give you to make you feel better," she said, kissing the hand that continued to pat her cheek. Marty had gone to visit her sister for a few hours after lunch.

Rosie whispered, "Pancakes."

"Yes, Marty makes pancakes." Breezy pushed the recliner with her feet. "But it isn't breakfast, sweetheart. Maybe fruit would be good."

"Fruit is good," Rosie said, leaning her head against Breezy's shoulder again.

Violet was sound asleep now. Rosie, from the looks of things, would be joining her. And what in the world should Breezy give them to make them feel better? Fever reducer, maybe? She leaned her cheek against Rosie. She did feel a little warm. She hoped they wouldn't be sick for the Christmas celebration at the end of the week.

She heard the rumble of a truck coming up the driveway. The flash of dark blue meant Jake was home. She leaned back, relieved. Because he was there to help with the twins. She told herself that had to be the reason she ached to see him.

It couldn't be more. Because more meant putting everything on the line, opening herself up to pain, to rejection. It had been a long time since she'd wanted to take the chance.

Right now, with the twins counting on her, with a new life and new opportunities, maybe it wasn't the right time. It might be better to be content with friendship.

As she rocked and the twins slept, she told herself that she had to draw the line between herself and Jake. Friendship. Anything else and they risked hurting the twins. And that was the last thing she wanted to do, to have a broken relationship with Jake that would hurt Rosie and Violet.

Jake walked into the living room a few minutes later. When his gaze immediately slid from her face to the twins, it grew concerned.

"Are they sick?"

She nodded. "Just a cold, I think."

He leaned down, touching his lips to Violet's head. "She feels warm."

"I know. If you're going to be here for a little while I'll run in to town and get medicine. Marty isn't here but I know Oregon or Wanda, at the grocery store, can point me in the right direction."

"Let me help you get them into bed." Jake reached for Violet. Even in her sleep the little girl reached for him, wrapping her arms around his neck.

As Breezy stood, she allowed herself a quick look at Jake. He'd dressed for business in dark gray dress slacks, a light gray button-down shirt and black boots. He smelled expensive, the kind of cologne a girl notices. Something a touch oriental but all masculine.

She must have made a sound because he gave her a cautious look. She widened her eyes at him and went all innocent.

"Something wrong?" he asked.

She shook her head, situating Rosie against her shoulder. "Hmm, not that I can think of."

Other than the fact that he made friendship a very difficult task.

She followed him to the room that belonged to the twins when they stayed at the Circle M. Jake placed Violet in the crib and stepped back for Breezy to settle Rosie next to her. The twins curled against each other. Breezy covered them with a light blanket.

"I have something for you," Jake said as they walked back to the living room. It had grown overcast and the room was shadowy but sparkled with lights from the Christmas tree.

"For me?"

He held up a finger. "Stay here."

She waited while he disappeared into the kitchen. A moment later he was back. He handed her a box.

"Is it for Christmas?" She shook it just slightly.

"No, you can have it now."

She slowly pulled the red foil paper off the package. Inside was a cardboard box. Jake pulled a pocketknife out of his pocket and slit the tape. She looked up at him and then at the box, lifting the flaps to look inside.

Her eyes filled with tears as she pulled out a glass ornament. On one side it had the year. On the other side was a picture of Breezy with the twins. A picture Jake had taken a little over a week ago as she and the twins made cookies.

"It's beautiful." She held it up, studying the picture, the happy looks on their faces.

"Are you crying?" He grabbed a box of tissues off the coffee table.

She took one and wiped her eye. "I'm not crying, I'm just… I'm touched. And I want to hug you."

"Hugging leads to kissing." He grinned as he warned her. But she saw that, like her, Jake meant to keep this limited to friendship. And of course they should.

"I know, but this…" She put it back in the box and set the box and the tissues on the table.

She took a step toward Jake, not really thinking about repercussions. "Why?"

He traced a line down her cheek to her chin with a finger, and tilted her face so that her eyes met his. She melted at the touch.

"Because I know that it's important to you to feel as if you belong here. I've watched as you've collected your ornaments, decorations, plants and even recipes. I'm not sure why those things mean so much, but I know they do."

"They mean staying," she explained. "I've lived my life leaving things behind. Friends, dolls, pictures and books."

If she had these small things, it was proof that she would stay and not have to leave anything or anyone behind again.

"You won't have to do that ever again, Breezy. This is your place now, your community and your family."

She nodded, wishing she could believe it as easily as he said the words. Maybe collecting those things was her way of convincing herself. His finger had dropped and now he held her hand. He pulled her a little closer and she looked up at him as he leaned to brush a sweet kiss across her lips.

"You won't have to leave it all behind," he assured her.

She loved the thought behind his words. She

loved the idea that she would always be here. But she knew that Lawton's will stipulated that Jake, if he ever saw reason, could undo her guardianship. He could take the twins from her.

He could break her heart.

Jake watched as Breezy left to go to town. She'd withdrawn after he'd kissed her. She'd told him again how much she loved the ornament. She'd picked it up and carried it out with her. Probably because she wanted it on her tree. It symbolized something for her. All of the things she'd collected, even the puppy Oregon had promised, symbolized putting down roots.

He went to his office, flipping on the light as he entered the room. He knew what worried her, or at least he thought he did. The thing they both knew was in Lawton's will: the stipulation that Jake could remove her from guardianship.

Jake also knew what Breezy wanted to keep hidden and what probably haunted her every day. He picked up the private investigator's report. He'd hired the man before Breezy had showed up. He'd wanted a way to protect the girls. Now he felt that old weight bearing down on his shoulders. The need to also protect Breezy.

Lawton had done that, had put her in his care. It might look like joint custody, but it was also

Lawton's way of keeping his sister safe, and of giving her what she should rightfully have had.

Jake tossed the paperwork in the trash. A few petty crimes, a mistake that anyone could have made, it was all history. She deserved to have her past left in the past. Didn't everyone?

If she'd trusted him enough to tell him, he would have explained to her that no one should have their past weighing down on them. He knew, because he'd allowed his to be a weight around his neck for too long.

But she didn't trust him. He got that. Trust didn't come easily to someone like Breezy. She'd never really had anyone she could trust. Her mother had never protected her. Her father hadn't acknowledged her. Maria Hernandez had never given her the basic necessities. And now she had to trust that he wouldn't take her nieces from her.

Somehow he had to assure her that wasn't going to happen.

Breezy went back to her place before going to town. The medicine for the twins was her main reason for going to Martin's Crossing, but she had another. It was cold and Joe would be out in this weather. As she drove into town, she came in from a side road onto Main Street.

When she saw him, it took her by surprise.

He was at the end of the block, standing by a light post that was wrapped in twinkling red lights. He was obviously watching Oregon's shop.

Breezy pulled up and rolled down the passenger window of her car. "Joe?"

He looked away from Oregon's shop, unsmiling and lost.

"Joe, are you okay?"

He wiped at his eyes and cleared his throat. "Of…of course I am."

"Can I do something for you? It's going to be cold tonight and I thought maybe we could find somewhere for you to stay." She handed him the thermos of coffee she'd prepared at her place. He took it in his gloved hands.

"You're a kind person, Breezy. Back a few weeks ago when Pastor Allen asked what our faith means to us, I think you were searching."

"Yes, I was searching," she admitted.

"But I think you're figured out what your faith means. Its more than all of this." He swept his arm in a wide arc. "All of this is pretty. It makes people happy. But without faith, it's just empty lights and tradition."

She watched as he poured himself a cup of coffee and she didn't know what to say. She agreed, faith was more than tradition. But traditions helped people remember their faith.

"Joe, you can stay at my place."

He shook his head. "I don't think Jake Martin would appreciate you opening your home to me, Breezy. But that's very kind of you."

"Joe, you can't stay outside tonight."

"I won't be outside." He took a sip of the coffee. "Very good coffee. Thank you."

"You're welcome, and I know you won't be outside. I know you're sleeping in the nativity."

He chuckled, his eyes twinkling in the dim light of late afternoon. "It's warm. The light is a heat lamp. I think Pastor Allen did that on purpose. And there's a soft bed of hay behind Mary and Joseph."

"That's all very cozy and nice, but it isn't a home."

"Breezy, don't worry about me. I'm making up for my past."

"The past doesn't have to hold us prisoner. If we believe what we say we believe, then aren't we set free? Isn't that the purpose of that baby in the manger?"

"Whom the Son sets free is free indeed," Joe quoted. "Yes, Breezy, you're right. I've been set free from my past, from the many things that nearly destroyed my life. But I have something I have to do, and until it's done, I'll be staying in the nativity. If it was good enough for that baby, it's good enough for me."

How could she argue with that? "If you change your mind…"

"If I change my mind, I'll let you know." He winked, held up the coffee in salute and walked away.

Breezy watched as he made his way back to the nativity. She wondered how no one else had noticed that Joe slept there every night. But then, no one else had really been watching. They were all trying to figure Joe out, wondering if he was safe, where he'd come from and when he'd leave.

They had no idea that Joe was making their lives better.

Breezy considered him a friend.

After picking up the medicine for the girls, she headed back to the Circle M, worrying that Jake would wonder what had taken so long. She thought of Joe and his determination to make up for the past. She was just as determined to let go of hers. Maybe letting go meant telling Jake?

When she pulled up to the house, she saw Jake waiting on the front porch. She got out of the car and held up the bag of medicine. Jake walked down off the porch to meet her. A caged lion came to mind. He looked as if he'd been pacing.

"I'm sorry. I saw Joe and I wanted to make sure he's okay. It's going to be cold tonight."

"I know it is." Jake took the medicine from her. "But you should have called. I was worried."

"Are the twins still sleeping?"

"Yes, and Marty's making dinner. Breezy, I'm serious about this. You need to understand that until we prove who has been breaking into the house or catch them, you're not safe."

She slipped her arm through his. "I know. And I'm sorry. But you also have to trust that I'm being careful. I'm not going to put myself or the twins in danger."

"But you went to your house."

"Just to get coffee for Joe," she admitted.

"Next time, don't. Or at least let me go with you," he said.

"Right, okay. I do have to go over there tomorrow. There's a horrible smell in the fridge. Something has to go."

Right, okay. Just make sure you activate the alarm while you're in the house."

"Yes, sir. I'll activate the alarm," she agreed, teasing him. He mock-scowled at her.

It was nice to have someone worrying about her. But it was still a new feeling to Breezy, and she was afraid to get used to it.

As they stood in the living room, the lights from the tree twinkled. Christmas was just around the corner. Somehow they would make this work. They would make a family out of the remnants and they would survive.

## Chapter Fifteen

Breezy left the girls with Marty when she drove over to her place the next afternoon. Jake had been out in the barn, talking to Brody about some cattle the younger Martin wanted to buy. They'd been at it for hours and she hadn't bothered to let Jake know she was leaving. Marty knew. And Breezy would keep her promise and set the alarm.

As she walked in the front door, she answered her phone. It was Joe.

"Hi, Joe, what's up?"

"Am I speaking to Breezy Hernandez?" It wasn't Joe's voice.

"Yes, this is Breezy." She turned to push a code into the alarm and then waited to close the door and make sure it was activated.

"Miss Hernandez, I'm calling from Austin Community General. We have a patient, Joe

Anderson. He asked us to call you and let you know that he's here. He's had a heart attack and he's in serious but stable condition."

"Joe?"

"Yes, ma'am. Mr. Anderson wanted someone to know."

"I'll be there as soon as I can."

She hung up and stood there for a minute. She wasn't sure what to do. Did he have family? Was he alone? She would go to him, of course. Everyone deserved to have someone. A person to call, to turn to.

She walked through the house, uneasy. She really disliked that someone had taken her peace, her joy in living in this house. It was her home. She had a plant. She had a nativity. And she was getting a dog. That's what people did when they had a home.

The fridge was her main goal for the day. That and more clothes. She opened the fridge door and held her breath, grabbing contents and tossing them in the trash. Something really stunk.

A noise caught her attention. She told herself it was nothing. And then she tried to convince herself it would be Jake coming to check on her. But Jake would have announced himself. He wouldn't be in the office and that sound definitely came from the office.

Slowly she closed the refrigerator door. She opened a cabinet drawer and pulled out a rolling pin. Anything could be a weapon. She eased along the wall, taking careful steps. As she walked she reached into her pocket for her phone and came up empty. She'd left it on the table in the living room.

Wonderful.

Go after the prowler or get her phone? The phone. And the alarm. She eased across the living room and as she reached for her phone he came running. She hit Redial, knowing it would ring to the ranch.

"Might as well hang that up," he said. He was tall with blond hair. She didn't know him but he looked like someone you would say hello to on the street.

"Who are you?"

He smirked. "What does it matter?"

"Well, if you think you're going to hurt me, I'd like to know the name of the man I'm going to knock out," she informed him with what she hoped was a confident look.

"Aren't you going to wait for Jake to rescue you?"

"No, I typically don't wait for a man to rescue me. You're in my home and I'll handle you," she said. "And your name?"

"Tyler Randall, the man who should have had

twenty percent of a business, not ten. But you managed to get my share. You showed up, and claimed to be the senator's daughter."

"I never made the claim. Lawton found me and…"

He waved his hand in the air. "I don't really care. I'm just letting you know—" he raised a file "—that I'm getting what is rightfully mine."

"And you think I won't stop you?"

"I think unless you want Jake Martin to know that you were arrested on suspicion of murder, you won't say a word."

She froze, looking at the phone in her hand, hearing Marty yelling, asking if she was safe. Her breath came in ragged gulps. How could she be okay? Someone knew. And if he knew, Jake would know.

And she would lose the twins.

"Oh, I've upset you." Tyler Randall took a step toward her. "I have an idea. You sign your share of the business over to me and I won't tell Jake that the aunt of his nieces has a criminal past. Of course there's a chance his P.I. will eventually uncover this information, but for now you'll be safe in your stolen life."

Her stolen life. She shook her head. It wasn't stolen. It was hers and it was real and it meant everything to her. The twins meant everything to her.

Jake. She let go of the pain that threatened to steal her breath. He had hired a private investigator. He hadn't trusted her. She couldn't let that be a distraction, not now.

"I'm not signing anything over to you. I'm calling the police." She raised the phone. Marty was still talking, still trying to convince her help was on the way. She pushed End and called 911.

Tyler rushed her, but she stepped to the side. Maria hadn't been a perfect parent but in little ways she had shown she cared. She had made sure Breezy could protect herself.

"You won't get away from me." Tyler laughed, not as confident as he'd been a minute ago.

He reached for her and she grabbed his arm, kneed him and then elbowed him in the nose. He went down on his knees, screaming in pain.

"Self-defense, Mr. Randall. I'm not anyone's victim."

She had been once, a long time ago. But she would never be a victim again. She pushed him down on the floor and held him with her knee in his back as a car roared up the driveway. When Jake walked through the door, she stepped away.

He nodded and then he jerked Tyler to his feet. There were sirens in the distance. It was over.

She walked out of the living room, leaving

Jake to clean up the mess. On her way out of the room she looked at the nativity on the mantel. In the kitchen she walked past the poinsettia she'd watered and cared for. It stood two feet tall and was covered with red blooms.

Jake could now effectively take the twins. Why would he be loyal to her? She was the sister who came out of nowhere to claim a portion of Lawton's life, his inheritance, his children.

He had hired a private investigator. That knowledge hurt. Where trust might have been, she now had the knowledge that even as they'd been forming their own family with the twins, he'd been looking for a way to take that family away from her.

As the thoughts rolled through her mind, she knew they weren't logical.

Logic didn't seem to matter when nothing made sense. Her heart feeling shattered didn't make sense. Her anger didn't make sense.

What made sense was leaving. She had to go to Joe. He needed a friend and she could be a friend. As she headed for her car, Jake caught up with her.

"Where are you going? The police need to talk to you," he said.

"I need to go."

"Breezy, you can't leave. You can't just walk

away." He reached for her hand. "Come inside and talk to the deputies."

"Right, okay."

"Why do you think you have to leave?"

She blinked a few times. "Because I'm always going to be the homeless girl in your eyes. You are never going to trust me, not completely."

"We need to discuss this."

She shook her head. "No, I need to talk to the deputies. Just let me get this over with. The one thing I can't do is talk to you right now."

"So you want me to back off?" he asked. "When have you ever backed off and left me alone? You forced me to admit that everyone needs someone. You need someone right now."

"You hired a private investigator," she accused. Pain tightened in her throat and tears burned her eyes.

He didn't deny it. "I had to protect the girls."

"Right, of course. Now I have to talk to the police and then I have to go. I have a friend and he needs me."

He put his hands up and backed away. "Fine, go talk to the police."

She nodded and walked past him, pretending she didn't need him.

Jake wasn't going to argue with her. He wouldn't chase her and plead with her to stay in their lives. No way would he tell her how much they needed her.

He remembered trying to tell his mother they needed her. He'd pleaded with her to take Samantha and Brody, to not leave the little ones. She had shaken her head and told him she was sorry. She couldn't stay and be a mom.

The police questioned Breezy. She told them everything Tyler had confessed to. She told them how she'd defended herself. And then she thanked them and said she had to go.

She walked over to the Christmas tree and took her ornament off, the one he'd given her. When she approached him she did so with her chin up, her brown eyes soft. She looked like a woman preparing herself for a battle. "I'm leaving. It's easier than waiting for you to tell me to go. But I'm taking this. I'm not leaving everything behind. And I'd like to be able to see my nieces from time to time."

He should stop her, he thought. But he couldn't. That twelve-year-old boy who had begged his mother to stay wouldn't let him. If people didn't want to stay, they couldn't be forced.

"Take whatever you want."

She opened her mouth as if she meant to say something, but she shook her head and walked away. He watched her as she got into her car and drove away.

Jake turned back to the house. Tyler was being put in the back of the police car. The deputy gave Jake a few more details. They would follow up, letting Jake know what charges would be filed. Jake listened but his mind had drifted off, to the pain that flashed in Breezy's eyes.

He should have told her about the private investigator. He should have told her it didn't matter. Not anymore. But he'd waited too long and someone else had told her. No matter what he said, he looked guilty. He looked like a man who didn't trust her.

When he pulled up to the house, Marty came out. She watched him walk up the steps, across the porch. She stepped aside to let him in the house. "Well?"

"She's gone." He kicked off his boots.

"What do you mean gone?"

He brushed a hand across his face. "What does gone usually mean?"

"In this household it means a stubborn man doesn't know what's good for him and didn't fight to keep what he wanted."

Jake plopped down in the recliner and looked up at her. "Really? And what does this man want?"

"That woman?"

"I'm not going to chase after her and try to force her to stay."

"No, you wouldn't want to do that. Why try to talk out a misunderstanding when you can let it hang between you? After all, words are so useless." Marty shot him an accusing look and then she dusted the table with the towel she'd carried in with her.

"I learned a long time ago that you can't beg someone to stay in your life."

"You learned that, did you?" Marty sat down on the edge of the sofa. "Did you ever learn that sometimes a person needs to hear the truth so they can make an informed decision?"

"I've learned that, but I also know that Breezy is not a woman who stays in one place long. Maybe she was looking for this out?"

"I don't think so. She loves it here and she loves those girls." Marty let a hefty pause hang between them. "And I think she probably loves you. Although I'm not sure why."

"Must be my charm."

"Go after her."

"I don't know where she went," he admitted. "Maybe she went back to Oklahoma. If so, then maybe that's where she wants to be. Her sister's there."

Marty studied him for a moment. "What's in that report?"

"That's her business to tell."

"Do you care about her?"

Jake shrugged at the question. "I've known her three weeks. I don't know what I feel."

"Oh, I think you do."

Maybe he did care for her, but he'd been wrong before. What if he was wrong again?

# Chapter Sixteen

Breezy walked down the hospital corridor to a room at the end. The nurse had informed her that Mr. Anderson was in a private room. And then the woman had said that Joe was quite a charmer. Yes, Joe was. But a private room? She thought back so many years ago and shivered at the memories.

For a long moment she stood outside the door of Joe's room telling herself that this moment was nothing like Maria. Joe wasn't going to die. The nurse had told her that he'd definitely improved and that he was now stable. Though it had been touch and go when the ambulance had brought him in.

Ambulance? What had Joe been doing in Austin?

There were a lot of questions and only the man himself could answer them. She rapped lightly on the door, waited for him to invite her in, then peeked inside the room to make sure it was indeed the Joe she knew. He waved her inside.

"Joe, how are you?"

"I'm going to be just fine, Breezy. It's this old ticker of mine. It hasn't been the healthiest the past few years. I never expected it to knock me down, though."

He indicated a chair next to the bed. She looked around the room with the small sleeper sofa, recliner and even a dorm-size refrigerator. It was better than the apartment she'd lived in back in California.

"This is nice, Joe. Much better than the nativity," she observed.

"If the nativity was good enough for the King of Kings, I think it is good enough for one old man who has done a lot of wrong things in his life."

"Joe, is there someone I can call?"

"No, there's no one."

"No family, no children?" she pushed.

He brushed a neatly manicured yet shaky hand over his face and shook his head. "No, I think not."

Now she was confused. "You think you don't have children or you think I shouldn't call?"

The nurse came in, took vitals and checked

the IV. She then moved around the room to take care of other small tasks and then asked Joe if he would like some coffee. Joe pointed at Breezy.

"No, but my guest might."

Breezy shook her head. The nurse smiled at them and left.

"Joe, are you sure you're okay?"

"I will be. It's just time for me to make things right."

And then Joe told her a story about a young man who had come from a good family, a wealthy family, but he'd had a drinking problem that no one but his wife knew about. He'd been a mean drunk, he admitted. And his wife, rightly so, had left him. She'd taken their child with her, and a good deal of his money. She'd also forced him to sign paperwork stating he would never try to see their child.

"I'm so sorry, Joe." What else could she say? "But why were you living on the streets in Martin's Crossing? Judging from this room, you don't have to be homeless."

"No, I don't have to be. I chose that life for the past year. I guess you could say I'm a senior citizen runaway."

She smiled at that. At least Joe had options.

Joe reached for her hand, patting it in a fatherly gesture. "I'm sorry for worrying you."

"It's okay." She removed her hand from his. "Joe, you're the one who has been helping people out, aren't you?"

"You won't tell, will you?"

She shook her head. "No, I won't tell."

"Thank you. I'm going to rest now. And you don't have to stay. I know you have those little girls and Jake Martin. I wouldn't want them to worry."

She didn't bother telling him she didn't think Jake would worry about her. He was probably looking at the guardianship papers right now, wondering how to take the twins away from her. But she wouldn't let him.

She wouldn't let him break her heart. And she wouldn't let him take Rosie and Violet from her. She wouldn't allow him to take the life she was building for herself.

"Are you still with me, Breezy?" Joe's voice, gravelly with sleep, broke into her thoughts.

"I'm here. I'll step out for a moment."

"You don't have to stay," he argued.

"I'm not leaving you alone."

She had left Maria. Even now it hurt to remember how it had felt to leave her. Breezy had been nineteen when it happened. She'd found a day job and on her way back she'd seen the ambulance, the police, the crowd on the street corner where she had left Maria that morning.

Maria had insisted. She'd planned on selling papers, hoping to make a little extra money so they could get a room. But rooms didn't come cheap.

They said someone had taken the money and pushed her. Breezy went to the hospital that evening and she'd stood a short distance away from Maria's room, gathering the courage to go inside, to say goodbye to the woman that had raised her. Instead the police had found her and taken her into custody. They'd questioned her about Maria, about why she had run when she saw the police. They'd questioned her about where she came from.

Why had she run? She'd been afraid of the police, but how could she explain that? Maria had taught her to never trust them or give them information.

Standing in the hall of this hospital it was easy to remember that young woman and how alone she'd felt when the police had told her it was too late. Maria had passed away from a heart attack she suffered during the mugging. Later they allowed her to leave the police station because they'd determined that she and Maria were family. They'd even driven her to a shelter for the night.

She sat in the bed at the shelter, alone, afraid and unsure of how she would live the rest of her life with no family, no home and no real education. She had even tried to remember Mia's last name, because Mia had taken care of her when they'd been children, hiding from their mother and her string of boyfriends.

Pushing the past away, she called Jake. Not to give him explanations but to tell him she would be back. She loved the girls and she wasn't leaving.

When he answered the phone, she hesitated.

"Breezy, where are you?"

"I'm still in Texas. I'll be home in a day or two."

"You're okay?" He actually sounded concerned. She wanted his concern. His friendship.

Silly heart. It had soaked up his friendship like a dry sponge soaks up water. It had wanted more than a plant, Christmas decorations and a puppy to prove it belonged in Martin's Crossing.

"Breezy?"

"I'm here. I'm just…"

"I'm just going to ask one thing of you. Don't walk out on these little girls. They need you."

"I'm not walking out. I don't walk away, Jake." She closed her eyes and did her best to not cry. "Don't take them away from me. I know that you must know about Maria, but I can explain it better than a private investigator."

"We'll talk about that when you get back."

"Okay. Thank you," she whispered at the end of the conversation.

The call ended. At least he hadn't said he would take the girls from her. That was something. She stood for a long time leaning against the wall, her eyes closed, her heart feeling squeezed. Eventually she took a deep, shaky breath, opened her eyes and told herself she would get through this. She always survived. She always managed to get back on her feet. This time would be no different.

Jake avoided looking at Brody and Duke as they brought in the cattle they needed to work before bad weather hit. Breezy had been gone for two days. They didn't know exactly where or what she was doing. And Duke was none too happy. If Jake cared to explain, he could have told his brother he wasn't too happy, either.

The twins weren't happy. They'd already lost enough. They didn't need to lose Breezy. He should have kept his focus, not allowed himself to get distracted. By her. After all of these years of keeping his priorities straight, he'd dropped the ball when the twins needed him focused.

"Hey, get that heifer," Brody yelled. "Jake, are you anywhere near this farm?"

Jake shot his little brother a meaningful look as he kneed his gelding and the animal shot around the cow that had been trying to make a break for it. He circled her, bringing her back to the herd.

"I got her." He gave Brody a pointed look. "And I don't need your…"

"Could we not fight?" Duke interrupted.

"Not fighting," Jake said. "But you know, this job should have been done months ago when these calves were easy to handle. Not now when we're going to have to run them in a chute plus deal with mommas that don't want their babies taken from them."

"So it's my fault you're in a bad mood?" Brody flashed him a look that was a little too confident and went after a rangy steer that was trying to head back to pasture.

"Yeah," Jake growled, "it's your fault."

Duke laughed, pushing his hat back a smidge as he rode up next to Jake. "You know you're just mad because you've never been good with the ladies and this time, when one was handed over to you like a Christmas present, you let the past get in the way."

"I…"

"Her past and yours," Duke continued.

"This has nothing to do with the past." Jake eased up on the reins when his horse started tossing his head. "Could we just get these cattle in the corral?"

So they did. The herd moved through the open gate. Brody jumped down and closed them in, limping a little.

"You okay, little brother?" Duke asked.

Brody nodded as he flung himself back into the saddle, gathering up the reins and turning his horse toward the barn. "I'm good. But thanks for asking. I'll get the stuff."

"Don't forget the rubbing alcohol," Jake called out after his retreating back.

"I never do," Brody half snarled.

"You have to stop treating him like a kid. He's twenty-six, not fifteen." Duke pulled his right leg loose from the stirrup and hooked his knee over the saddle horn.

"Then he needs to act twenty-six."

Duke shook his head. "Stop being the parent, Jake. That's half your problem with Breezy. You like her, but you won't let yourself because you're punishing every woman for Sylvia's crimes."

"I'm not punishing anyone," Jake insisted.

"Yeah, you are. You're even punishing yourself. You think you have to take care of the whole family and half the town. After all, Mom left, Dad left. Who does that leave in charge, the noblest of creatures, Jake Martin? Stop."

Jake leaned forward in the saddle and pointed at Duke. "You think I don't want to stop. But how do I stop when I have two little girls who now need me to raise them."

"Get yourself a wife. Loosen up a little and enjoy life. When was the last time you went on a date?"

"I don't date."

Duke pointed at him. "That's right, because Sylvia left, so how can any woman be trusted? If I was you, and I was this twisted up inside over a woman, I'd try to get her back."

"She's coming back," Jake admitted. Man, he was exhausted. He wished Duke would let it go. But as much as Jake thought he had to take care of their family, Duke thought he had to keep them all hugging and smelling the flowers.

"Why aren't you happy about that?"

"Duke, this isn't a relationship. Breezy and I are raising the girls together. End of story. Maybe for a little while I forgot that. I might have crossed lines I shouldn't have crossed."

"Jake Martin crosses lines?" Duke whistled. His horse sidestepped and Duke, even though he didn't appear to have control, brought the horse back around with no problem.

"Breezy and I are going to have to sit down and discuss our relationship."

"Why don't you just date the woman, Jake?"

Jake leaned to open the gate and rode through. "We have work to do."

"Yeah, there's always work to do. Why don't you answer my question?"

Jake eased his horse through the gate and Duke followed. They knew what to do without actually discussing it. They would separate calves from mommas long enough to take the calf through the chute, give him his immunizations and tag his ear.

Brody had walked back to the corral. He had a bucket with the tags, alcohol, giant-size needle and everything else they would need. Yeah, he was growing up. Whatever had happened between him and Lincoln had hurt him, but Brody wasn't a kid anymore.

"Jake, you didn't answer me."

"I don't want to answer you. I want to get this work done. I have Christmas shopping to do and some other errands to run."

And he didn't want to explain that anything more than friendship could ruin things not only between himself and Breezy but also for the twins. The twins had to be his priority.

For now and forever.

# Chapter Seventeen

It took Breezy ten minutes to find a parking place. Martin's Crossing just days before Christmas was a busy place. She hadn't realized it would be like this, that the entire town would show up for this early Christmas celebration. Down the block she could see the parade lining up. The floats were lit with Christmas lights. A school band was warming up.

She stood next to her car waiting for Joe to get out. He'd been released from the hospital that morning. They'd gone to his home so that he could pack a few things. It had surprised her, Joe having a home.

He joined her and they walked across the street and down the block to the park. In the distance a horse whinnied. Of course there would be horses in the parade. Breezy scanned the crowd looking for Jake and the twins. She ached to see them. But she was afraid.

"You'll be okay, Breezy. And so will those little girls."

She put a hand on his arm. "Thank you."

The church choir was warming up. They would be singing outside because the weather was good. Breezy, with Joe at her side, walked toward them. She didn't know if she would still be included. Her acceptance here had a lot to do with her acceptance by the Martins. She knew that. And she wanted their continued acceptance.

She wanted this Christmas to be special. It would have been if she hadn't crossed lines with Jake. If she had remembered that relationships never worked in her favor.

No, she shook her head as she chastised herself. This Christmas would be special. She had a home, she had Rosie and Violet. And she had friends in Martin's Crossing. She would have a big dinner and invite Oregon, Joe and anyone else who might be alone for the holidays.

A flat trailer was being used for a stage. Breezy headed that way. Margie spotted her. The older woman called out and waved Breezy forward. The others noticed and many of them called out, friendly smiles on their faces.

"Breezy, I was so worried you wouldn't be here for your solo. But here you are. And Joe, too. I'm so glad to see you both." Margie gave

Breezy a quick hug and then handed her a song-book. "We'll sing right after the parade and then before cookies and warm drinks in the commu-nity building."

"Okay." Breezy held the songbook and glanced around. "Have you seen the twins?"

"They're with Marty. I saw her pushing the stroller. Those little girls have grown, I think," Margie said. "You go catch up with them and we'll see you after the parade."

She drifted away. Joe had left her. She knew that he planned on helping serve cookies and drinks. Like her, he had found a place in Mar-tin's Crossing. She hoped, no, she prayed that things went well for him in the future.

As she walked toward the street she spotted Marty and the twins. She called out and Marty turned. Breezy stopped, waiting to be beckoned forward, waiting for Marty's reaction. The older woman smiled and waved. Something eased in-side Breezy.

She hurried forward, catching up with them as Marty positioned the stroller so the twins could watch the parade. The girls spotted her and started to cry her name. But garbled in the word *Brees,* she also heard *Mama* and she knew that she wouldn't leave. Jake would have to make the decision to take away her rights to the twins. And she knew he wouldn't.

They would work out a way to be friends. They would spend Christmases together for years to come. So this year was important. She had gotten off track with wishful thinking. But she was back on track now. She would be able to smile at Jake and pretend nothing had happened.

She would pretend he didn't shake her world to the core.

"Rosie, Violet." She kneeled next to the girls and gathered them in hugs, kissing their cold cheeks. Rosie patted her face and Violet pulled herself out of the stroller to cling to her neck.

"They missed you." Marty said it with a kind look that didn't include censure. "I missed you, sweetie."

Those words meant everything. With both girls clinging to her, Breezy stood and allowed Marty to take her, with the twins, into a motherly hug. She breathed in, fighting the sting of tears.

"It's good to be home," Breezy said as she backed away, wiping at her eyes.

"You're okay?" Marty asked as she moved them all toward the street and the approaching parade.

"I'm good. Joe was in the hospital so I stayed in Austin long enough to bring him home."

"Breezy, you had quite a shock with Tyler

Randall coming after you the way he did. I wish you hadn't left."

"I just needed a few days," Breezy explained. "And I'd gotten the call about Joe. I had to go to him."

"I know. We have all the time in the world to talk. But I want you to know you have people here who care about you."

She nodded, fighting tears. Marty sighed and patted her arm.

The parade was almost to them. At the front was a local band with only a dozen or so students. They played "Silent Night" as they marched past. Young girls carried the banner with the school name. The twins waved and bounced in Breezy's arms.

Breezy set the twins down. She held Violet's hand and Marty held Rosie's. Breezy pointed so that the girls could pick up the wrapped pieces of chocolate and lollipops that were tossed to the people lining the street.

For thirty minutes they stood there watching. The floats from area organizations and churches came after the horses. Another band, this one playing "Joy to the World," walked by.

More candy was tossed and the girls would pick it up and hand it to Breezy to put in her pockets.

Near the end came the local saddle club. Jake,

Duke and Brody road with them. Breezy held her breath as she made eye contact with Jake for the first time in several days. And it still hurt. His lack of trust hurt.

At the very end, the local fire department had decorated their old truck with lights and music blasting from speakers. Santa sat in the back. The truck stopped and more candy was tossed.

The crowds pushed closer, gathering more candy. Children rushed to greet Santa. Someone pushed close behind Breezy and she stiffened, waiting for an attack that didn't come.

"It isn't a big parade, but it's always been one of my favorites." The voice, low and husky, came from behind her.

Breezy hesitated before facing Jake, hoping she didn't look too desperate. "It has been fun."

"Welcome home."

"Yes, it's good to be back. Where's your horse?" she asked as she and Marty put the girls back in the stroller.

"Duke put him in the trailer so I could get over here to the girls. And to you."

"They loved the parade."

"I thought they would. They're old enough to enjoy these things a little more. Last year…"

She touched his arm. Last year his sister and Lawton had been here.

He cleared his throat. "Last year they were barely a year old."

"A lot changes in a year," she said.

"Yes, a lot changes."

"I need to go join the choir." Breezy looked down at the twins again. It was easier to focus on them than the man with the crystal-blue eyes standing in front of her.

"We'll be over there in a minute." Jake took the stroller from Marty. "I drive slower than Marty."

She managed a smile and walked away. For the twins she could do this. She *would* do this. But it was going to hurt. No two ways about it.

Jake ignored the look Marty gave him. The one that asked him what he was going to do. He didn't have an answer, and he didn't want to think about this. Not tonight.

It was hard enough that today he'd caught Brody on the computer searching for Sylvia Martin. He'd told his kid brother to let it go. He'd tried to find her once. He'd written her a letter when their father died. She'd responded and told him she was really very sorry and hoped they were all doing well. He tried to write and tell her they were great without her. That letter was returned, undelivered.

He had to acknowledge that Breezy wasn't

Sylvia. Breezy had come back. As hurt as she was, he knew she would come back to the girls.

"Jake, you have to find a way to make this work. For the twins." Marty touched his hand as he pushed the stroller. He stopped pushing and looked at her, trying to find an answer for her and for himself.

"I will." Jake let the words out on a sigh. "I made a mistake, but I'm going to fix it."

"What mistake? Being attracted to Breezy?" Marty winked as she said that. "I can't see how you two falling in love is a mistake. Not for you, for her or the twins."

"I don't think I mentioned love," he said. "I meant I should have told her about the P.I."

"Yes, you should have."

The band played a few notes, warming up. Jake watched Breezy take her place on the makeshift stage. She stood up there in her long skirt, sweater and boots, blond hair down her back. She belonged. To this town. To him.

Man, he wanted to push his way through this crowd of people and take her in his arms. But he couldn't because he didn't know what he was feeling or what would happen come next week or next month.

Marty whispered for him to move forward and stop staring because he looked like a fool.

He chuckled and shook his head. He pushed the stroller forward, joining the crowds.

"Lawton wanted us to become a couple," Jake shared with Marty.

She laughed. "He was your best friend and he wanted you as happy with his sister as he was with yours. Makes perfect sense to me."

"Not to me. Take two people with trust issues, toss them in a situation and see what you get." He walked around to the front of the stroller and handed Violet the drink she'd asked for.

He missed his sister at times like this. And he missed Lawton. He pushed his hat back and took in a deep breath and let the pain out on the exhale.

The music started, giving him a much needed reprieve. Marty was as bad as his brothers these days, wanting to involve herself in his life. His relationships.

The choir started to sing. "Away in a Manger" came first. They included a choir of children for this song, letting the little ones sing the last verse without the band. The crowd's silence said everything. Especially since tonight the baby Jesus had been put in the nativity and the star above the little building was lit.

The last song of the night included Breezy's solo. He watched as she sang "Mary, Did You Know?" Their gazes locked for an instant, then she glanced away, her eyes widening on something or someone behind him.

Jake spun around, worried it was Tyler Randall, even though Tyler's bail was high and Breezy looked thrilled, not upset. A couple approached Jake, and a small boy of about seven walked with them. The woman was tall with long dark hair. The man next to her wore a cowboy hat and a protective glare. Family, Jake guessed.

The woman walked up to him, pinning him with a look.

"Jake Martin, I'm Mia McKennon. Breezy's sister."

He must have looked perplexed because the man next to her held out a hand and offered an apologetic look.

"Slade McKennon, and you'll have to overlook my wife. She's retired from the DEA but she hasn't retired from digging into other people's business." He gave his wife a look that Jake couldn't miss. He brought the boy up to his side. "This is our son, Caleb."

"It's good to meet you." Jake shook Slade's hand and then watched as Mia knelt next to the twins, her smile for them a lot different than the one she'd given him.

"Breezy didn't know we were coming down,"

Slade offered in a way that seemed to be another apology.

"Didn't she?" Jake said. Breezy was still on the stage. They were singing "Hark! The Herald Angels Sing." The crowd sang along.

After the song ended, Slade McKennon spoke again. "No, she didn't. Mia talked to her yesterday and said she got a bad feeling. Mia doesn't ignore her bad feelings. And I guess I've learned not to ignore them."

"I see," Jake said. He got the distinct impression they thought he was responsible for those bad feelings in Breezy's life.

As he watched Breezy hop down off the trailer, the only thing he could think about was loading her up in his truck and taking her for a drive somewhere, far away from all of these people and their opinions.

If they drove far enough, maybe they could outrun both of their pasts.

He'd like to hold her close as they sat on the tailgate of his truck watching stars. It had been a long, long time since he'd done anything like that. He couldn't remember the last time he'd even wanted to take a woman for a drive down by the creek. He wanted to hold her hand, maybe brush a kiss across her knuckles. He wanted like crazy to tell her that if they could be friends, maybe they could be more.

But all of those thoughts fled like darkness come sunrise. Breezy's family had come to check on her, to make sure she was safe. What did they want after that? To take her back to Oklahoma?

Breezy hurried toward them. When she reached them, she pulled her sister into a hug, reaching for the boy, Caleb, as she did. The two sisters talked, laughed, hugged again.

Violet started to cry. Breezy broke away from her sister as she gave Violet her attention, leaning down to pick up the little girl who wanted to be held.

"They're beautiful," Mia said. Her hand, probably without her realizing, went to her belly. "I can't believe that by summer I'll have a little person like that."

"Maybe a little smaller." Breezy smiled as she said it, holding Violet to her shoulder.

Rosie, not to be left out, looked at Jake with big tears falling down her cheeks. He picked her up and she immediately reached for Breezy.

"I think they've missed you," he said.

"I could take them tonight. If you think..." Breezy shrugged.

"That would be good." Jake handed Rosie over. "I have some shopping to do tomorrow. By the way, if you haven't seen Lilly, she wanted me to let you know the puppy is weaned."

"Right, Daisy. I'll pick her up tomorrow."

"I can pick her up on my way home and bring it to your place," he offered.

"Okay, thank you, Jake."

"Mia and Slade are welcome to stay and join us for Christmas." He made the offer and Marty nodded her approval, then motioned that she was going to the fellowship hall for cookies.

Breezy looked at her sister, hopefulness in her expression. He knew she missed Mia. He knew this had been hard for her, being tossed into the lives of strangers.

"Of course we're staying," Slade answered, his arm sliding around his wife's waist. Caleb moved to the spot in front of his dad and Slade's hand rested on the boy's shoulder.

Jake gave the other man a cursory nod, then he looked at Breezy. "I'll see you tomorrow."

Breezy stepped forward. Her sister had taken Rosie and she had Violet in her left arm. With her free right hand she touched his cheek and then she stood on tiptoe and kissed where she'd touched.

"I'm sorry, Jake."

She really knew how to bring a guy to his knees. He didn't think she realized how she twisted him inside out. He didn't think she had a clue that he was fighting the urge to kiss her in a way that would show her that friendship just wasn't going to work.

He just stood there, watching as she stepped back, a sweet expression on her face.

"I'm sorry, too," he said. As soon as he could he would offer a real apology for the private investigator, for not trusting her.

As he stood there thinking about how to make amends, she walked away with the twins, a boy named Caleb, her sister and her brother-in-law. They looked like family.

And oddly, he felt like the outsider.

Breezy and Mia stayed up long after the twins, Caleb and Slade went to bed. They curled up on the couch with herbal tea and talked about home. Mia's home in Dawson, her family the Coopers, the Mad Cow Café where Breezy had worked and all of the other people Breezy had known while living in that small Oklahoma town.

"Are you homesick?" Mia asked.

Breezy had to think about that. She missed Dawson. But it would hurt Mia's feelings to tell her it hadn't been her home. It had been Mia's home, Mia's family and friends. Breezy had felt somewhat settled there.

"I do miss it," she admitted. "I miss you and your family."

Again, they were Mia's family.

"But?" Mia set her cup on the table next to the sofa and pulled an afghan up to her waist.

"This really does feel like home. I miss you all, but I'm supposed to be here. I'm supposed to raise Rosie and Violet. I keep thinking about how Lawton came into my life when he did. What if he hadn't found me? What if I'd never known him? I would have missed out on so much."

She wouldn't have known her brother. She would never have known who her father was. She wouldn't have had the twins. It would have been Jake raising those little girls alone.

And she missed him so much. Even though she'd just seen him, she missed *him*.

"So about your parenting partner," Mia started with a knowing look, her mouth turning slightly and her eyes twinkling. "He's easy on the eyes."

"Yes, he is." There was no denying it.

"And the two of you are close?"

"Do we have to go there?" Breezy sipped her tea and dragged part of Mia's afghan to her own feet.

"Yes, we do. I'm worried about you. I'm worried that he is going to break your heart."

"He won't break my heart. We know what we need to do."

"And what's that, Breezy?" Mia jerked the blanket back to her side and grinned. They had missed out on so many moments like this because Maria had taken Breezy away. They had just found one another, just started to get reacquainted, and then Lawton had found Breezy.

But their reconnecting didn't have to end. They could visit, talk on the phone and share pictures. Breezy would definitely be with Mia when she had the baby.

Mia nudged Breezy with her foot. "Come back to earth."

"Jake and I have to be friends for the sake of the twins."

Mia barked a laugh and then covered her mouth with her hand. "That's hilarious. Friends, for the sake of the twins. There's electricity between the two of you. You look at each other and forests in other states catch fire."

"That isn't true."

"Oh, it's true," Mia said with a grin. "And if you think you can contain that in a mason jar like a lightning bug, you're fooling yourself. There's no lid tight enough to hold in that force. I know because I fought my feelings for Slade for a long, long time."

"I know."

Slade's wife, Mia's best friend, had died in a

car accident. It had taken Mia a long time to be okay with what she felt for Slade.

"I want you to be happy, Breeze. You deserve to be happy. And to have this awesome home. And stuff to fill it with." Mia grinned and lifted her cup to her lips.

Breezy looked around the house, at the things she'd bought to make this house her home. She wouldn't leave it. She wouldn't take off in the night and leave behind the things she loved, the things she cared about.

She wouldn't leave Jake behind. Or the twins. Because when she thought of things she couldn't leave behind, it wasn't material things at all. It was the people she loved.

And she loved Jake Martin.

## *Chapter Eighteen*

Christmas morning dawned and Jake was awake. He made coffee before Marty came to the kitchen to start cooking. She kissed his cheek and went to work on the meal that would feed their family. She could have gone to visit family in Austin or San Antonio, but she considered the Martin kids her kids. She had told him last night that she really wouldn't want to be anywhere else.

He was glad she felt that way. He knew without a doubt that they wouldn't be nearly as functional without her.

He plugged in the lights on the tree and the lights on the mantel while he waited for everyone else to wake up. And he waited for Breezy, the twins and Breezy's family. They would be there within the hour.

"I'm going to run out to the barn to take

care of a few things." Jake walked through the kitchen on his way to the back door.

"I'll have breakfast ready when you get back. Over easy?"

"Yes, thanks," he called out as he headed out the door.

When he got to the barn he stopped to check on Breezy's Christmas gift. He was kind of proud of himself. He hoped Breezy would like it as much as he did. He planned on giving the gift to her here, in the barn. He wanted time to talk to her. Alone. He wanted time to explain that he'd been wrong and he wanted to make things right.

Her brother-in-law's truck was in the drive when he got back. He found them all in the kitchen, seated at the bar stools around the counter. Caleb, Slade's son, was wearing a cowboy hat today and what appeared to be new boots.

"Nice boots, Caleb." Jake leaned down to take a look.

The kid began to tell him all about the boots and how they were the best. Jake tousled his blond hair before stopping to see the twins, who were sitting on Breezy's lap. They were barely awake. Rosie rubbed a hand over her eyes and smiled up at him. And then she raised her arms in a silent request. He picked her up, holding her close.

"Have you been in the living room?" he asked.

Breezy shook her head. "No, we didn't want to give anything away."

"Good. I want to see their faces when they see…"

Breezy cut him off, a finger to her lips. "Shh, don't tell them."

"You know, it's all I could do not to come over last night and get them so they could have their gifts," he admitted.

Slade laughed at that. "Caleb got a new saddle and we gave it to him two days ago. I couldn't wait."

Mia gave her husband a sweet look. Jake thought that look said it all when it came from a woman like Mia, who appeared able to take down small armies if necessary.

"We could take them now," Breezy offered.

"No," Marty said in a loud, firm tone. "Breakfast, then gifts. New parents always get ahead of themselves."

Jake looked at Breezy and saw it register in her expression. That moment when they realized this was it. They weren't going to wake up tomorrow and have this all be a dream.

She reached for his hand. He'd missed her.

Brody walked into the kitchen a few minutes later, rubbing sleep from his eyes and then smoothing hair down with his hand. He might be an adult but he still looked like a kid who woke up on Christmas morning half-asleep but ready to open gifts.

"Breakfast," he muttered.

Caleb took a long look at him. "You're a bull rider."

Brody narrowed his eyes and looked at Caleb. "Did we get another kid?"

Caleb laughed at that. "No, I'm Breezy's nephew. Those are my parents. They kiss a lot. Grown-ups do that when they love each other."

He said the last part as if repeating what he had been told often.

Jake wished the kid would stay around a little longer.

Brody looked at Caleb, one eye squinting. "So you're the new sister's nephew. I guess you can call me Uncle Brody. And yeah, I used to ride bulls."

"You don't ride bulls anymore?" Caleb continued to quiz even though Mia had put a hand on his arm.

Jake watched the exchange, interested in things Brody didn't really say to any of them. And yet he'd tell a kid he barely knew.

"No, I don't ride anymore." Brody grinned. "But I'm finding other things to do."

Duke showed up next. Caleb eyed him as he walked through the door. The kid's eyes widened. Duke poured a cup of coffee and hugged Marty, who handed him a plate of food. Everyone else was eating.

Everyone but Caleb. He spun in his chair to watch Duke take a seat at the table. "Are you a giant?"

Duke spooned a mouthful of eggs into his mouth. "Yeah."

"Cool."

Everyone laughed.

After breakfast they all walked to the living room. The twins held Jake and Breezy's fingers. They had been little last year and Christmas hadn't been like this, filled with awe and wonder.

Christmas music played on the radio and the smell of ham baking filled the air. Rosie and Violet stopped in the living room, their eyes widening at the sight of the tree and all of the gifts.

They had put the rocking horses under the tree with ribbons around their necks. Jake had bought some type of scooter for Caleb. It would work great in the driveway, the salesgirl at the toy store had told him. When Caleb saw the scooter he just looked at it.

Jake grinned at the boy and indicated with a nod that he should head for the tree with the twins. "I think you'll find something with your name on it, Caleb."

Caleb took the twins by the hand and led them over to the tree. The girls climbed on those rocking horses and Caleb pulled the scooter out to give it a thorough look.

Jake put Brody in charge of handing out the other gifts. As he did, their other guests arrived. Joe, Oregon and Lilly. He watched as Lilly immediately went to Duke, showing him the ring she'd gotten from her mom and telling him how much money she had saved in her piggy bank for a horse.

Joe took a seat next to Marty and asked if she'd like some help in the kitchen. Jake saw Marty's cheeks turn red. Joe had secrets, but it was no secret that he was charming.

As things settled down, Jake walked up to Breezy. She looked up at him with a soft smile playing on her lips. "Merry Christmas, Jake."

"I have something for you," he said. "If you could escape for a few minutes."

She looked at the twins. They had unwrapped gifts and were busy on the floor with their new dolls. Next to her, Mia gave her a little push.

"Go. I'll watch them," Mia offered.

The day was cool so Jake handed Breezy a jacket from the hook at the back door. They walked outside together. He reached for her hand. As they walked, he wondered if this was the right gift, at the right time.

He'd soon find out.

Breezy hadn't expected more gifts from Jake. He'd given her a wooden box from Lefty's shop filled with family recipes. He'd also given her a bracelet with pretty charms and jewels. The gifts were sweet gestures of friendship.

Now he said there was more.

"Where are we going?"

He shrugged. He didn't answer.

"Jake?"

"Do you understand what a surprise is?"

She sighed and continued to walk with him, trudging across the crunchy, frosty ground. They reached the barn and she wondered if maybe he had given her boxing gloves. That would be nice. She'd like to hit something.

He led her through the barn, turning on lights as they went. A horse whinnied. Jake didn't say anything. Why didn't he say something?

"Are you going to give me a hint?" she asked.

"No need." He put his hands over her eyes and turned her. When he removed his hands she faced a stall. And in the stall a pretty golden horse with an almost white mane and tail stood watching them, its golden ears pricked forward.

"What?"

"It's a horse," he said, close to her ear. She could feel the warmth of his breath. She could almost sense his lips close to her cheek.

"Yes, a horse." She reached and the animal nuzzled her fingers.

"Merry Christmas, Breezy."

She turned to look up at him, awed, unsure. "You bought me a horse?"

"I'm hoping you're happy. I was really going for happy."

"Of course I am, it's just… I didn't expect a horse." A horse belonged to someone with roots, someone who stayed. She wanted a horse and all it implied.

He pulled her close. "That's the wonderful thing about a surprise. It's unexpected."

Yes, unexpected. Like Jake. "You didn't trust me."

He sighed. "I should have told you about that report. I started all of that before I met you. And then I didn't know what to say, how to tell you."

"You could have asked me to tell you what happened."

"I know," he admitted.

"So what do we do now?" She waited, knowing that she loved him more than she'd ever expected to love anyone. How did she keep boundaries when her heart had already made up its mind?

"I think we should agree that Lawton made a good decision and he knew what was best for the twins."

Her heart quaked a little because she didn't know what that meant. "Okay."

"Breezy, you're the best friend I've ever had. I don't want to lose you."

She pushed her hands through his hair and brought his head close to hers. Face-to-face she stood on tiptoe, touching her lips to his. "And yet, you make friendship more…"

He kissed her long and sweet, her arms around his neck.

"I make friendship more…?" he leaned in to her.

"More complicated. More interesting. More difficult. I'm not sure what we're supposed to do now."

"I think that what we do now," he said, "is move forward."

She waited, knowing there had to be more. Her heart needed more.

"I know you've left a lot behind, Breezy. I think you've left more than people and possessions. You've left pieces of yourself."

"Oh, Jake." Had anyone ever gotten it the way he did?

"I love you and I want to put all of our pieces back together and make us whole. Together."

She placed a hand on each of his cheeks and pulled him down, touching her lips to his. "Thank you."

"I messed up, Breezy. When you first came I was in a panic, trying to protect the girls. Protect my family. And I let you down. I didn't trust Lawton. And I didn't trust you. I should have."

"I think we couldn't have imagined this happening." She raised the hand she held and brushed her lips over his knuckles. "I love you, too. I'm not going anywhere. I want to be here. I want to be in your life and in your arms."

"That's where I plan on keeping you, Breezy."

"Forever?"

"Yes, forever."

He kissed her again. It was a slow, lingering kiss, the kind that made them forget the barn, the horse, the people waiting inside. Slowly they returned to themselves, and Jake took her by the hand and led her back to the house for Christmas with the family.

*Their* family.

# *Epilogue*

Breezy loved Martin's Crossing. She loved it in the winter when Christmas lights decorated the entire town. She loved it in the spring with trees budding, flowers blooming and warm air reminding everyone that winter never lasted forever.

She realized that hard times were like winter. They sometimes seemed like they would go on forever, but they never did. Spring always came with sunshine and the promise of better days.

On a pretty day in late April, with flowers blooming and birds singing, she waited in a small classroom at the Martin's Crossing Community Church. Somewhere out there, Jake was waiting for her.

She smiled at her ladies-in-waiting, as she liked to call them. The Coopers were all present to help with wedding preparations. Mia was her matron of honor, even though she was due to give birth in a matter of weeks. Oregon was a bridesmaid. The twins were flower girls. Breezy thought the flower petals would end up everywhere but where they should be sprinkled.

"You look beautiful," Marty said as she arranged the veil. Marty was taking the place of mother of the bride. And she was happy to do so, as she had no children of her own.

The twins had recently started calling her Gamma.

"And the dress?" It had been Mia's wedding dress, and Breezy loved that they could share it, and share this occasion. A few years ago she hadn't dreamed of having a family. Now she had it in abundance. When God provided, He didn't skimp.

"Perfect," Marty concurred.

Heather Cooper handed her a bouquet of white and pale pink roses. "There's a guy out there, in the church. He has the sweetest smile."

Mia chuckled. "And we thought it would never happen."

Heather shot her a look. "Nothing has happened. I just wanted to know his name."

The door opened. Lilly ran through the room straight to her mother. She spotted Breezy and stopped to stare. "Wow, you're beautiful. I think my mom should marry Duke so I can be a bridesmaid…"

Oregon shot her daughter a look. And Breezy thought it wasn't the typical mom-embarrassed-by-daughter-talking-too-much look. It was a look of fear.

Mia must have noticed it, too, because she took over.

"I think we should probably find out if Jake is ready for his bride."

Lilly quickly volunteered and ran out the door. Breezy smiled down at the twins in their pale pink dresses. Caleb was the ring bearer. He was with the men.

Breezy winked at Oregon. Oregon didn't smile. Instead she looked as if she might cry.

But it was too late to ask questions. Lilly was back and informed them that it was time. Breezy walked out the door of the room and down the hall to the back of the church where Tim Cooper, Mia's dad, was waiting to walk her down the aisle. He smiled at her, patting her hand as she placed it on her arm.

The music started, and Breezy took a deep breath and prepared herself to meet the man she loved at the front of the church.

She loved him. She smiled at the memory of the night he'd asked for her hand in marriage, while slipping a ring on her finger. It had been

Valentine's Day and they'd cooked dinner together at her place. She'd turned around and he'd stepped close behind her, waiting for that moment to pull her close.

"I love you," he had said as he'd kissed her. She'd seen the walls coming down, the trust growing. She'd known. God had known.

He'd seen two damaged people and He'd used faith, love and a little time to put them back together. He'd made a family out of those broken people and two little girls. He'd taught them to trust themselves—and to trust Him.

Today she would marry Jake and they would continue to build a new life, a new family.

Mia and Slade walked down the aisle ahead of her. Slade stepped behind Jake at the front of the church. Mia took her place to wait for Breezy.

Duke waited for Oregon to take his arm. She did, but didn't look at him.

And then Tim Cooper walked Breezy down the aisle. She beamed at Jake as she walked toward him, whispering that she loved him. He mouthed the words back to her.

Yes, they had gotten this right. She stepped next to him. Tim kissed her cheek and wished her all of God's blessings.

Pastor Allen recited the vows, words of honor, of love, of standing strong through good times and difficult times. During a quiet moment while they lit the candles, Breezy thought about all of the ways God had blessed her.

Pastor Allen then brought them together—Jake, Breezy, Violet and Rosie. "Breezy, this is your family. God has entrusted them to your care." He looked at Jake. "And, Jake, you have been given this wonderful blessing. A wife and two little girls. With everything else in life that you do, everything that keeps you busy, always remember this—this wife and these children are the most important thing God has given you to do."

Jake looked at Breezy, smiling as he held her hand. Rosie and Violet wandered off. The people in the church laughed softly as the girls went their own way, sprinkling flowers in their wake.

Pastor Allen cleared his throat and then he continued.

"Jake and Breezy Martin, by the power vested in me by God and the state of Texas, I now pronounce you husband and wife. Jake, you may kiss your bride."

Everything in her life had led her to this moment. She moved into her husband's embrace and he kissed her. She melted in his arms.

They left the church to a cheering crowd and music that celebrated love. When they reached the car that would take them to a resort a short distance from town where they would have a reception, someone shouted that she should throw the bouquet.

She paused, looking back at the crowd of people gathered to celebrate their wedding. A large group from Oklahoma had traveled to Martin's Crossing for the wedding. Not only the Coopers, but also Vera and several others. All of them mixed in with her family and friends from Martin's Crossing.

Tears gathered in her eyes as she saw this united bunch of people. They symbolized everything that had changed in Breezy's life. She had a place of her own. She had family.

A hand tugged on hers, reminding her of the most important change in her life. She had Jake Martin's love, and together they would raise their twin nieces.

She would build a life and a family here in Martin's Crossing. With a smile she tossed the bouquet, watching as women rushed to catch it.

Breezy smiled up at her husband and he leaned down to claim her lips in a kiss that would be hers, forever.

\* \* \* \* \*

Dear Reader,

Welcome to Martin's Crossing, a fictional town in Texas Hill Country. I'm so excited about this new miniseries. New characters, new romances and new places to visit. But I couldn't change locations without taking a few familiar characters.

In A Rancher for Christmas, Breezy Hernandez moves to Texas where she finds a home, a place to belong and a man who loves her unconditionally.

I hope you enjoy your stay in Martin's Crossing!

Merry Christmas!

*Brenda Minton*

# Questions for Discussion

1. Breezy's life changes overnight. How can she find faith and contentment in those changes? How does faith make a difference in facing difficult situations?

2. Jake has to trust Breezy with the lives of his nieces. Facing this unknown, how does he react?

3. Breezy lived a life of instability as a child. How does this affect the way she faces situations as an adult?

4. Jake helped raise his siblings and still feels responsible for them. How can he let go? What would you do in his situation?

5. Jake has to learn to trust that Breezy won't leave. He is judging her for her past and also for the way his own mother walked out. How are his feelings legitimate? How are they wrong? Have you judged others for what someone else has done?

6. How are the traditions of Martin's Crossing important to them as they celebrate Christ-

mas? What traditions do you have that make the holidays special for you and your family?

7. Joe is a mystery to the townspeople. They are both reluctant to accept him and yet willing to include him. Why is that important?

8. Why is putting down roots so important to Breezy? What does community mean to you?

9. Breezy and Jake have been changed by the circumstances of their lives. How? How does the past affect you? How do difficult times change us?

10. Jake has to learn to let someone else help out once in a while. Why is that difficult for him to accept? Is it hard for you to let people help?

11. When does Breezy realize that she's in love with Jake, and that her future is in Martin's Crossing?

# LARGER-PRINT BOOKS!

## GET 2 FREE LARGER-PRINT NOVELS PLUS 2 FREE MYSTERY GIFTS

*Love Inspired®*
## SUSPENSE
### RIVETING INSPIRATIONAL ROMANCE

### Larger-print novels are now available...

# REQUEST YOUR FREE BOOKS!
## 2 FREE WHOLESOME ROMANCE NOVELS IN LARGER PRINT
## PLUS 2 FREE MYSTERY GIFTS

✻✻✻✻✻✻✻✻✻✻✻✻✻✻✻✻✻✻✻✻✻✻✻
### HEARTWARMING™
✻✻✻✻✻✻✻✻✻✻✻✻✻✻✻✻✻✻✻✻✻✻✻
*Wholesome, tender romances*

---

**YES!** Please send me 2 FREE Harlequin® Heartwarming Larger-Print novels and my 2 FREE mystery gifts (gifts worth about $10). After receiving them, if I don't wish to receive any more books, I can return the shipping statement marked "cancel." If I don't cancel, I will receive 4 brand-new larger-print novels every month and be billed just $4.99 per book in the U.S. or $5.74 per book in Canada. That's a savings of at least 23% off the cover price. It's quite a bargain! Shipping and handling is just 50¢ per book in the U.S. and 75¢ per book in Canada.* I understand that accepting the 2 free books and gifts places me under no obligation to buy anything. I can always return a shipment and cancel at any time. Even if I never buy another book, the two free books and gifts are mine to keep forever.

161/361 IDN F47N

Name _____ (PLEASE PRINT)

Address _____ Apt. #

City _____ State/Prov. _____ Zip/Postal Code

Signature (if under 18, a parent or guardian must sign)

### Mail to the Harlequin® Reader Service:
**IN U.S.A.:** P.O. Box 1867, Buffalo, NY 14240-1867
**IN CANADA:** P.O. Box 609, Fort Erie, Ontario L2A 5X3

HWDIR13R